SIGH FO[...]

Lorimer women are not to be trusted!
Betrayed by one Lorimer six years ago,
surgeon Griff Rydell has neither forgotten
nor forgiven his suffering. And when
theatre nurse Kelly Lorimer appears at
Porthbryn General, he makes it quite
clear that this time he's *not* going to fall
under the family spell . . .

SIGH FOR A SURGEON

BY

LYNNE COLLINS

MILLS & BOON LIMITED
15–16 BROOK'S MEWS
LONDON W1A 1DR

First published in Great Britain 1984
by Mills & Boon Limited

© Lynne Collins 1984

Australian copyright 1984
Philippine copyright 1984

ISBN 0 263 74964 9

Set in 10 on 11½ pt Linotron Times
03–0285–55,000

Photoset by Rowland Phototypesetting Ltd
Bury St Edmunds, Suffolk
Made and printed in Great Britain by
Richard Clay (The Chaucer Press) Ltd
Bungay, Suffolk

CHAPTER ONE

THERE WAS something familiar about the tall figure of the man who walked slightly ahead of her along the windswept promenade . . .

Musing, Kelly huddled deeper into the protection of the anorak she wore over a thin shirt and well-washed jeans, grateful for its warmth. A fine start to summer, she thought ruefully, as the wind whipped her long fair hair about her face to stinging effect and the sea lashed savagely at the wooden groynes along the shore and grey clouds lowered on the skyline. Here and there, a few early holiday-makers scowled and shivered as they braved the elements, trailing dogs or reluctant children.

He *was* familiar, she decided abruptly, an odd *frisson* rippling unexpectedly down the length of her spine. There was something she knew in the set of that dark head and the nape of the neck with the crisp black curls and the brief glimpse she caught of a very handsome profile as he turned towards the sea. Strong nose, proudly jutting chin, bronzed good looks.

He was very tall, lean and lithe but powerfully built with those broad shoulders, and he walked with a very slight drag of the long left leg. Perhaps it was the limp that she'd noticed first. As a nurse, it was the kind of thing that she would notice, of course. As a woman, she studied that familiar back and handsome head with a different kind of interest, trying to place him, wondering if he might be a patient she'd nursed during her years at Hartlake.

But she *did* know him, she decided with a sudden

flutter of her heart as recognition dawned. It wasn't just imagination.

Impulsively, she quickened her steps to reach him and clutched at his arm. 'Griff . . .?' she demanded, smiling, eager with surprise and delight. 'Griff Rydell?'

Pausing, he looked down that very handsome nose at her, a frown in his steely grey eyes, rebuff written all over the attractive face. For a moment he considered her unemotionally, expressionless. Then, coolly, he disengaged her fingers, discarded them.

'I don't believe I know you.'

Kelly felt a stirring of doubt but she persisted. 'I'm Kelly Lorimer . . . Kate's cousin! Oh, you don't remember me, I suppose?' She laughed, understanding, not minding. 'I expect I've grown up!'

He didn't smile. His eyes hardened slightly. 'You are mistaken,' he said stiffly, wondering what *she* was doing in Porthbryn, where he'd settled down happily in the hope of never seeing Kate or any of her family again.

Kelly was disconcerted. Had she made a mistake? It was almost six years, after all.

'I'm sorry . . . I thought you were someone I used to know . . .' It was lame and she broke off, embarrassed, moving out of his path.

With a curt nod that acknowledged the apology, he walked on. She stood irresolute, looking after him, puzzled and slightly dismayed. *Had* she accosted a total stranger? Wouldn't a stranger have smiled, shaken his head in friendly fashion, perhaps even murmured a polite and slightly regretful disclaimer that he didn't know the pretty girl who'd stopped him in his tracks?

Kelly *was* a pretty girl and it would be false modesty to pretend that she was unconscious of the impact of her blonde good looks on most men. But he hadn't shown the least flicker of interest in the heart-shaped face and wide hazel eyes and long, pale, flyaway hair that other men seemed to admire. He'd glowered at her and slapped her down so brusquely that she felt not only foolish but *cheap*.

She had a stubborn streak that showed itself in the slightly wilful lift to her chin and the way that her lovely eyes sparkled with militancy when she knew herself to be in the right. Now, her chin went up and her eyes narrowed and flashed with indignation as she looked after the receding figure of the man who'd denied that he was Griffith Rydell.

Having seen him closer, more clearly, face to face, Kelly just knew that he'd lied! At seventeen she'd fancied him like mad, although he'd been engaged to Kate and therefore out of bounds, even if he'd noticed that she was a woman and not just Kate's schoolgirl cousin. She'd only met him three or four times but he'd left a vivid and lasting impression on a susceptible young girl. So she'd never forgotten the striking good looks, the piercing, deep-set eyes with their crinkle of laughter-lines, the fall of rumpled black curls across his handsome brow or the way that his smile seemed to lighten the brooding attraction of his chiselled features, causing a girl's heart to tilt in her breast.

It had all been so youthful, so innocent, even slightly absurd in retrospect . . . those delicious, forbidden dreams of a man she scarcely knew. A man she'd almost forgotten, too, once the upset of Kate's broken engagement had died down.

Almost, but not completely.

Suddenly, Kelly ran after him again, determined. 'Excuse me! Just a minute . . . !'

It was so imperious that he halted, turned. Impatience was clearly etched in his lean, handsome face and there was a hint of irritation in the slight shake of his dark head. 'Well, what is it now?'

'You *are* Griffith Rydell, you know,' Kelly declared bluntly, oddly breathless and blaming a gust of wind for the impetus that had almost hurled her into his arms.

He raised a sardonic eyebrow. 'I'm obliged to you for the information,' he drawled, with frost in the grey eyes and the set of the mobile mouth.

'And you *do* know me,' Kelly swept on, almost angry, resenting his tone and the blank wall of his resistance. 'You nearly married my cousin!'

An elderly couple, walking their dog despite the chill wind and the threat of rain, glanced at them curiously as if they suspected a quarrel between lovers. The woman smiled at Kelly with a hint of sympathy and understanding and then murmured something to her husband.

'I'm *not* the man who nearly married your cousin,' Griffith Rydell said brusquely. '*He* didn't survive a car crash—and she wasn't interested in the man who did, you may recall. You force me to be rude but I've no desire to be reminded by you or anyone else of your cousin or what happened six years ago. It's over, forgotten. Now will you stop following me!'

Her face flamed. 'I'm not following you,' she said stiffly, proud. 'I happen to be walking in the same direction, that's all. I'm sorry I bothered you.'

Head high, she stalked ahead of him, feeling foolish, feeling humiliated—and feeling just a little bit sorry for him, too. For she'd been tactless and too impulsive in the way she'd rushed after him, thrust herself at him. She ought to have known that he wouldn't want to be reminded. How could he want to remember Kate and the dreadful thing she'd done to him? How could he want to know any member of Kate's family, in the circumstances?

Kelly walked quickly, escaping him. Feeling his gaze on her slim back, although she suspected that his thoughts had turned inwards and back six years. That he wasn't seeing her any more but Kate. Lovely, laughing Kate who'd hurt him so badly.

That limp was a legacy of the car crash, of course. So was the faint white line running from temple to jaw on the left side of that handsome face, clearly etched against the tan but only a pale shadow of the deep purple cicatrice of six years before, after emergency surgery. Kelly didn't feel it would be too fanciful to suspect that there were other, deeper, non-physical scars that the world didn't see.

He'd been in a wheelchair when Kate had said that she couldn't marry him, after all. No one, including the eminent neurosurgeon who'd operated on his injured spine, had been optimistic about his chances of walking again, leading a normal life, resuming his career. It had been too daunting for Kate, who wasn't even a dedicated nurse and couldn't face the prospect of spending her life caring for a disabled husband when she'd looked forward to marrying a fit young surgeon with a brilliant future.

Kelly had been sad about the broken engagement for his sake, but she hadn't condemned her cousin. It took a special kind of person and a rare kind of loving to take on a man who'd probably spend his entire life in a wheelchair, disabled, possibly embittered and certainly deprived in a number of ways. It wasn't Kate's fault that she'd lacked the love and the compassion and the strength of character that was needed in such circumstances. And it couldn't have been easy for her to admit that she no longer wanted to marry Griff or to endure the not always silent censure of family and friends.

Within three months she'd married someone else, and Kelly had sometimes wondered if she had done so because people were readier to forgive a change of heart for more acceptable reasons. Griff had been popular and everyone had been shocked and upset by what had happened to him and Kate's reaction, and perhaps she'd found it too uncomfortable to live under a cloud of disapproval because she'd let him down so badly and so soon.

Having married, Kate had left Hartlake Hospital and nursing and Griffith Rydell had become a part of the past that no one talked about, virtually forgotten by everyone. Including Kelly herself, studying for A-level examinations and looking forward to following in her cousin's footsteps at the famous teaching hospital.

Now, suddenly, in the strange way that life had of throwing up a thread from the past to colour the tapestry of the present, Griff Rydell had been forcibly thrust to the forefront of her mind by a chance encounter on a windswept promenade six years later.

Kelly wondered if he was on holiday or living in the area. Might they meet again—and would he continue to snub her, reject her, punishing her for Kate's fault? And did it matter?

Not at all, she told herself blithely, smiling at a small boy in bright red trousers and sweater and woollen balaclava who was digging happily in the wet sand, impervious to wind and threatening rain. She had a new job, new friends and new surroundings to think about and was no more interested in the past than a man who was little more than a stranger, anyway.

She dug her cold hands deeper into the pockets of her anorak and walked into the wind, heading for her parked car and deciding that she'd chosen the wrong day for exploring the sea front. It was so bleak and desolate that it chilled the spirits as well as the body—and there was something just as bleak and desolate about the man who walked in her wake, she decided, glancing at him as she reached the car and fumbled in her pocket for the keys.

His black curls were tossed and tumbled by the freakish fingers of the wind and he braced broad shoulders, a kind of anger in the grey eyes that glowered as he walked towards her, only that slight drag of the leg betraying that he'd once been threatened with a wheelchair for the rest of his life.

As a nurse, Kelly knew all about the miracles that could be achieved by medical science and surgical skill. But she was still surprised by the degree of his mobility, remembering how badly he'd been injured. More operations, she suspected, and years of physiotherapy and a determination not to be defeated. She wondered how Kate would feel if she met him now and saw how he'd overcome the threat of permanent disability.

She slid behind the wheel of her car and turned the key in the ignition slot. The engine refused to fire. The Mini was old and shabby and temperamental and it didn't like being left to stand on an exposed foreshore with a cold wind gusting about its bonnet. Used to its sulks, Kelly waited a moment or two and then tried again. Nothing happened. She sighed, tried once more and listened to the frustrated whine of the engine. She felt frustrated too.

Griff Rydell was reflected in the car mirror, just drawing level. Kelly thought he glanced towards the car, attracted by her obvious difficulty. She wound down the window on an impulse and called to him.

'Do you know anything about cars, by any chance?' He stopped with obvious reluctance, frowning. But he *had* stopped. Kelly took heart and smiled at him tentatively, willing to forget that earlier hostility. 'My car won't start,' she said unnecessarily.

He surveyed the small and somewhat battered vehicle and an eyebrow climbed into the tangle of dark curls on his brow. '*Is* it a car?' he asked sardonically.

Kelly wasn't sensitive. She'd been teased too often about her ancient car. 'So I'm told!'

He moved towards her, unsmiling. 'You do have some petrol in the tank, I suppose?'

She bridled at that. A typically chauvinist male, she thought crossly. 'Of course. I'm not an absolute idiot,' she said sweetly.

'Then it's probably a dirty spark plug. Or the points. Something fairly simple, I expect.'

It was indifferent, unhelpful. Kelly realised that he was about to walk on, to abandon her.

'Would you have a look at the engine for me? I'd be so grateful.' This time her smile was quick and warm and golden, the smile that had brightened many a patient's day and cheered many a young doctor when he was tired and jaded and full of doubts. It wasn't consciously potent, and that was the greater part of its charm.

Griff was unmoved by the smile that illumined a pretty face to near-loveliness and danced in her wide hazel eyes. 'Sorry. Your car looks and sounds as if it needs major surgery and I haven't the time or the knowledge or the inclination,' he said brusquely.

Kelly's eyes widened in dismay. In her experience, most men were only too willing to come to the aid of a damsel in distress and she hadn't expected a blunt and unfeeling refusal. Slightly flustered, she put the car into gear and tried the engine once more. The car started and shot back at speed. She'd put it in reverse! It was only a few seconds and a few feet before she slammed her foot on the brake but she wasn't in time to avoid a collision with the car that was parked behind her own. Kelly heard the bang and the tinkle of glass as the Mini hit the rear of a sleek, dark blue saloon that was obviously both new and very expensive.

'Oh, for God's sake, girl!'

There was so much anger and such despair of her sex in that heartfelt exclamation that Kelly looked at him swiftly and with sinking heart. 'Yours,' she said flatly. It wasn't a question.

'Mine,' he confirmed stonily.

'I'm so sorry . . .' What else was there to say to a man whose grey eyes were uncompromising chips of granite, whose mobile mouth seemed suddenly carved out of ice and whose tall frame was rigid with suppressed fury?·

'Back off!' he commanded. 'Let's have a look at the damage.'

It wasn't as bad as she'd feared. A smashed rear light and a dented bumper and one or two scratches on the brand new paintwork. Not the end of the world. But not the way to endear herself to any man, either, Kelly thought wryly. Men were so sensitive about their precious new toys!

'Women drivers are a damned menace,' he growled, stooping to inspect the damage to the bumper.

Kelly flushed. 'I've had my licence for three years and this is my first accident,' she said, instantly on the defensive.

'More through luck than judgment, I suspect.' He straightened to survey her small Mini. 'Your car seems to be relatively unscathed. No new dents and scratches to mar its pristine appearance.'

Her chin went up and her hazel eyes sparked fire at the scornful words and tone. 'You don't have to believe me, but I'm not responsible for the way it looks. It was battered when I bought it. All I could afford, and I haven't any money to spare on doing it up. Nurses aren't too well paid, you may remember!'

He regarded her thoughtfully. 'So you're a nurse, are you? Heaven help your patients if your nursing is anything like your driving!'

'It's hardly fair to judge my driving on a moment of carelessness!' she exclaimed hotly.

'A moment of carelessness can cause the loss of a life—or worse,' he told her grimly. 'Whether you're at the wheel of a car or responsible for the welfare of a patient.'

'Spare me the lecture!' Annoyed, Kelly briefly forgot what a moment of carelessness on the part of an unknown motorist had done to Griff Rydell and his life. 'I'm very sorry about your car and I'll pay for the damage, of course. I'll give you my address.'

She reached into the Mini, rummaged in the glove compartment and eventually found an old envelope and a pen and scrawled her new address. He didn't even glance at it, stuffing the envelope into his jacket pocket without comment. Kelly looked up at that handsome face with its unyielding expression and wondered if he hated all women because of Kate—or only hated her because she was Kate's cousin and she'd reversed into his new car!

'Will you forgive me if I buy you a drink?' she asked impulsively.

'That isn't necessary,' he said dismissively.

'No. But it's much more friendly than glowering at each other,' she returned lightly, smiling at him with unconsciously persuasive warmth.

He studied her coolly. 'Didn't your mother warn you against offering to buy drinks for strange men?'

Kelly chuckled. 'You aren't a stranger!'

'Nor a friend.'

It was so brusque that she felt snubbed. A flush rising, she wondered if he thought she was running after him. Smarting, she resorted to flippancy.

'Well, I wish I could say that it was nice running into you,' she said brightly. 'But I won't rub salt in the wound! You will send me the bill, won't you?'

'I doubt it.'

'Please!'

'We'll say that it was entirely my fault for parking so close to your car when I had a mile of almost deserted promenade at my disposal,' he said dryly, turning away with such an air of finality that it was obvious that he had nothing more to say to her on that subject or any other.

Kelly almost blurted that it seemed they'd been meant to meet. But he wouldn't appreciate the suggestion that destiny had played a part in the encounter, she felt. He hadn't been at all pleased to see her again—and even less so after she'd rammed his lovely new car!

He drove off without even a wave of his hand for Kelly as she stood looking after him. She hadn't seen Griff Rydell in six years and she would probably never see him again. So it was foolish to feel disappointed and vaguely hurt by his indifferent and unapproachable attitude. After all, she'd outgrown her youthful fancy for him long before, and it had been only an impulsive curiosity to know how he'd fared in the years between that prompted her to speak to him. Now, she could certainly dismiss him just as easily as he'd swept her aside, she decided with a proud tilt to her chin.

Driving through a sudden squall of rain, trying to familiarise herself with the lay-out of the Welsh seaside town, her thoughts turned to the new job. And Jeremy.

She'd been happy at the hospital in Kent where they'd met and she'd been in line for early promotion to Theatre Sister. But he'd persuaded her to join him at the recently built hospital in Porthbryn. They needed good nurses and she had all the right qualifications—and he missed her, he'd urged.

Kelly had missed him too, having worked with him and spent much of her free time with him for over a year. So she'd applied for a job at the Porthbryn General and got it. She would be working in the up to date theatre unit as a scrub nurse. She enjoyed theatre work and knew she was good at it, having been well-trained at a hospital with high standards and a fine reputation. The badge of a Hartlake nurse was an open door to some of the best jobs in the profession.

She'd gone so far to please Jeremy but no further, firmly resisting his suggestion that they should share the flat he'd taken near the hospital. She believed that he loved her but it rankled that he didn't mention marriage, although she wasn't at all sure that she wanted to marry him. She was fond of Jeremy. They were very good friends who enjoyed each other's company and had a great deal in common. But she knew instinctively that something was missing in her feeling for him and so she was reluctant to commit herself to an irrevocably intimate relationship.

She didn't want to live in, either. The nurses' home at the Porthbryn General was modern and comfortable and there seemed to be few of the old-fashioned restrictions that had chafed her set of first-years in the early training days at Hartlake. But she felt she would want to escape from shop talk and grape-vine gossip and the company of her fellow nurses after a long day in Theatres.

So, on a possibly foolish impulse, Kelly had followed up an advertisement she'd seen in the local paper and rented a tiny caravan sited in a farmer's field on the coast road just outside Porthbryn. She might regret it, but it was only for the summer and it had been ridiculously cheap and it would be an adventure, she'd defended her impulsive decision when Jeremy shook his head at her in amused reproach and declared that the place would be damp and inconvenient and that she probably shared the field with a herd of cows.

Moving in on the previous day, Kelly had been slightly disconcerted to discover just how small and cramped and primitive was her new home—and Jeremy seemed to be right about the cows! But the farmer and his wife were warm and kindly people, delighted to have let the caravan to a nurse from the new hospital up the road, and willing to be helpful in a number of ways.

The caravan was cosy, her very own domain, and the farmhouse was only a stone's-throw away. And the field bordered the road with its cluster of cottages and tiny shop-cum-post office and bus stop. The sea was only a hundred yards away down a tiny lane and the Welsh hills swept to the sky in the background. It couldn't be lovelier or less like the cold and clinical atmosphere of an operating theatre, and it would suit her very well, Kelly determined . . . as long as the sun shone occasionally that summer!

CHAPTER TWO

HEART beating slightly faster from a mix of excitement and trepidation, Kelly walked into the gleaming and aseptic theatre unit on the following morning to find the ever-reliable Jeremy waiting for her, his stocky figure garbed in surgical trousers and tunic, curly red hair almost hidden by a theatre cap and a mask dangling by its tapes about his neck.

'Survived another night in your sardine can, I see,' he greeted her lightly, blue eyes twinkling. His smile was warm and reassuring. He knew better than anyone else at the Porthbryn General that she had no need to be nervous. She was an excellent theatre nurse.

The teasing words dispelled her tension. 'I love it,' she said firmly. 'It's cosy and comfortable and it looks like home now that I've unpacked my things and scattered a few cushions and put your photo on the window ledge.'

'That should keep the cows away! They haven't invaded your privacy yet, apparently.'

'We had breakfast together and made friends.' She smiled at him. 'I'm shaking in my shoes,' she added in lower tones. 'I have that awful "new girl" feeling!'

But she couldn't feel that way for very long. Jeremy had paved the way for her too well and everyone was so friendly and welcoming that she was swiftly put at ease. She wasn't surprised to find that he was very well-liked. People always liked the good-looking, good-natured young surgeon with his mop of red hair and very blue eyes and cheerful willingness to please. Kelly liked him too, very much.

18

'Break her in gently, won't you, Angie?' he urged lightly, having introduced her to the tall and slender brunette who was the sister in charge of the unit.

Angela Howell had heard a great deal about the new theatre nurse in the last few weeks and she wasn't prepared to like her. Now, her brown eyes swept over the fair girl in the thin theatre frock in comprehensive and critical assessment, but her instinctive antagonism was concealed by the professional brightness of her smile.

'Oh, I won't ask you to scrub for any of my surgeons today, Nurse Lorimer. Finding your feet and getting used to my little ways will be enough for your first day,' she said generously.

Kelly tried not to bridle at the patronising note in the other girl's voice. 'I don't mind assisting right away, Sister,' she said quickly. 'I've had lots of experience of theatre work and I like to be busy.'

'And busy you will be, my dear. Never a dull moment in my unit. I'm putting you in charge of Number Two Theatre,' Angela told her briskly. 'We have four operating theatres and each is used in rotation so that every day one of them is thoroughly scrubbed and sterilised and prepared for the next day's list.'

'Yes, Sister. Thank you, Sister.' It was a demure and automatic response but Kelly's heart quickened with surprise and delight. For it sounded much more exciting than she'd been led to expect.

'You'll be responsible for everything, of course— instruments, gowns and gloves, drugs, sutures and dressing packs and much more that I'm sure I don't need to detail. You'll have two "dirty" nurses to help you and you'll scrub for the surgeons on each case allotted to your theatre, so you'll need to be well up on procedures . . .' She broke off, raising an amused eyebrow. 'You aren't turning pale at the prospect?'

Kelly laughed, shook her head. 'It sounds marvellous,' she declared warmly.

'Well, it's the way we do things here at the Porthbryn General. I'm in overall charge and always on hand if needed, but you'll be expected to cope without running to me unnecessarily. Some days you'll be rushed off your feet and other days will be more leisurely, depending on the list and how many emergencies come in. We take patients from a wide catchment area and we're the only Accident and Emergency hospital in the district. So we're always busy and it's vital that my staff know what they have to do and get on with it. But I'm sure you don't need a pep talk from me!' Her light laugh was for the benefit of the listening surgeon.

Kelly smiled dutifully.

'Jeremy tells me that you did six months in Theatres at Hartlake after you qualified and also that you were senior theatre nurse at Marks Cross for a year,' she swept on briskly. 'So you obviously have the kind of experience that will be very useful to us, Nurse Lorimer. I hope you'll enjoy working here, anyway.'

'Thank you, Sister. I'm sure that I shall.' Kelly wondered if the theatre sister was deliberately keeping her at a distance with that formal *Nurse Lorimer* while referring to Jeremy so easily by his first name. She was sensitive to the lack of welcome in the girl's attitude, for all the seeming pleasantness of smile and tone. Perhaps Jeremy had been too pleased about her advent and too enthusiastic about her various qualities for the attractive Angela Howell's liking, she thought shrewdly.

'Here comes your appendicectomy, Jeremy.' Angela indicated the trolley with its prepped and drowsy patient and escort of theatre porters and ward nurse as it emerged from a lift and was trundled towards the ante-room and the waiting anaesthetist.

'Yes. Mustn't keep a customer waiting.' He smiled and patted Kelly's shoulder. 'See you later, love. We'll have some lunch together if I get through my list in good time.'

Kelly looked after the surgeon as he pushed through the swing doors into the theatre, hurrying to scrub up and don gown and gloves for the first of the day's operations. Jeremy wasn't a brilliant or outstanding surgeon, but he was a very able technician who enjoyed his work and did it very competently.

Having assisted him so many times, Kelly liked the way that he didn't take himself too seriously. Some surgeons regarded themselves as next in line to God and expected to be treated accordingly and laid down their rules to be observed in the theatre. Some were temperamental and difficult and some were a real pleasure to work with, but all that she'd ever known had met with Kelly's genuine admiration and respect for their skill and dedication.

Every surgeon had his own likes and dislikes and his own way of working, of course. Jeremy had a deceptively light-hearted approach to his work, for instance, talking and laughing throughout surgery. But that didn't affect his concentration or his technique, although possibly it slowed him down slightly.

'I'm afraid there's no guarantee that you'll scrub for Mr Hunt very often,' Angela said briskly, crushing pretension. 'We have a team of surgeons and you may be working with any one of them according to the day's list.'

'Yes, so I understood at my interview, Sister. It wasn't just the hope of working with Jeremy that brought me to Porthbryn,' Kelly said firmly, dispelling illusion and underlining her friendship with the surgeon at one and the same time. 'It's a new and very up to date hospital, much bigger than Marks Cross, and I felt it would be valuable experience.'

Angela nodded. 'You know that it's a teaching hospital, of course? So you'll be training junior nurses in operating procedures, too. We've only been open for eighteen months so our first batch isn't yet baked, but we hope to turn out some very good nurses, even if we can't compete with the Hartlake reputation.' It was slightly acid.

Kelly had met with that hint of hostility towards her badge in the past. Hartlake nurses were considered to be among the best in the world, so it was natural that girls who'd trained elsewhere should resent the implication that they were inferior nurses. She sympathised, even while she secretly felt that few hospitals could attain the extremely high standards that Hartlake had set its student nurses for over eighty years.

She was shrewd enough to suspect that not all of Angela Howell's resentment was directed against her badge and she wondered just how friendly surgeon and theatre sister had become, on and off duty, in the few months that Jeremy had been working at the Porthbryn General.

'Sister . . . Telephone! It's A and E.'

The urgency of the summons couldn't be ignored. 'I'll get back to you later, Nurse Lorimer.' The slender and striking brunette hurried in the direction of her office.

Kelly set about acquainting herself with Number Two Theatre and her new and extensive responsibilities, including the two staff nurses who were already at work in the small but very well-equipped operating room.

Five years of nursing had taught her not only the job she loved but also how to get on with people of all types and temperaments. She realised that even the slightest hint of superiority in her attitude would be resented by the experienced nurses who would be regular members of her theatre team. She might be a very good nurse but so were they, for Porthbryn General was selective in its staff and that was only one of the reasons why it was rapidly earning a name for itself as an excellent hospital, despite its newness.

It might be that Kelly had considerably more experience of theatre work and its demands and had assisted at almost every kind of operation both at Hartlake and Marks Cross and that was why she had been put in charge. But it was an unexpected promotion and she hoped that her fellow nurses were happy about it and willing to work to her instruction. After all, few people cared for new brooms and she'd been suddenly thrust into a position of authority over long-standing members of staff.

She needn't have worried. Both girls were friendly and welcoming and glad to be relieved of a responsibility that had weighed heavily on their combined shoulders for the past few weeks. Sharon Lewis was a gentle, quiet-spoken girl who smiled but said little and Kelly was thankful to realise that her reserve was due to shyness rather than resentment. Megan Phillips was a plump and jolly girl who enjoyed the drama and urgency of theatre work but frankly admitted that she couldn't cope with a scrub nurse's job and didn't want to be in charge.

'Angie's a tartar when things go wrong,' she said cheerfully. 'Rather you than me on the receiving end of her scoldings in future!'

Kelly laughed. 'Between us, we'll see to it that things don't go wrong,' she said, light but confident, suddenly sure that they would make a good team. 'Now, I'll give you a hand and perhaps you'll tell me where things are kept and how things are done while we work.'

The unit was a hive of activity that morning and Kelly

saw little of the theatre sister, who was assisting a consultant gynaecological surgeon with his list. With the good-natured help of her new colleagues and the advantage of her previous experience, she was soon familiar with the lay-out and the working of Theatres. The atmosphere of quiet and controlled urgency and the familiar sights and smells and sounds were such as she associated with all operating theatres and she slipped so easily into the routine that by the end of the morning she felt as if she'd worked at the Porthbryn General for years.

The surgeons were rather remote figures in their green gowns and caps and masks, working steadily and with practised skill beneath the hot glare of the arc lights while the anaesthetist monitored and stabilised the patient's condition with his complicated array of equipment. Between cases, gowns discarded and masks dangling by their strings, they relaxed over cups of coffee and talked golf or cars or family matters. Then, coffee finished, they went into huddles to study X-rays and discuss technique or procedure or prognosis before the ritual of scrubbing-up began all over again with the arrival of the next patient.

Nurses moved quietly and methodically about their work, setting up trolleys and preparing theatres, replacing used instruments and providing fresh supplies of lotions or suture packs or dressings, counting swabs, cleaning and tidying after surgery. Other nurses received and reassured the pre-medicated patients on their arrival in Theatres and later looked after them and monitored their progress in the recovery room before they were returned to the wards.

Porters bustled in and out of the unit with trolleys and heavy items of equipment and gas cylinders and a great deal of light-hearted banter that dispelled tension.

Patients came and went via ante-room, operating-theatre and recovery-room, and the air was heavy with the smell of ether, aseptic lotions and strong coffee.

Kelly found time to stand and absorb the feel of the place and also to marvel at the superb efficiency of the girl who not only assisted demanding surgeons with delicate surgery but also ran a very busy unit without appearing to do so. The theatre sister was a very able organiser and she had a great deal of authority. She could delegate to good effect and she seemed to have a gift for sensing impending disaster and arriving on the scene at just the right moment to avert it. It wasn't an easy job by any means. But she made it seem easy and although Kelly found it difficult to warm to Angela Howell as a person, she had a great admiration for her work. She would do credit to a Hartlake badge, she decided, bestowing the highest accolade she knew.

Impressed by all she saw and heard, Kelly felt that she'd done the right thing when she had given in to Jeremy's persuasions and applied for a job at this modern and well-run hospital. She didn't know what the distant future held but for the moment she could be very content in the new job and new surroundings, she felt. There didn't seem to be a single fly in the ointment.

'You're in the way, Nurse!'

She turned at the snap of the words and then moved hastily aside to permit the passage of a trolley so surrounded by concerned staff that it was obviously an emergency. The patient was grey-faced—breathing stertorously and festooned with a variety of tubes and drips—and a nurse scurried alongside the trolley with a carefully held bag of plasma.

It was the kind of tableau that Kelly had seen times without number, but she looked after that one with suddenly quickened interest and an odd hop, skip and a jump of her heart. For it wasn't just that crisply peremptory voice that had been familiar, she realised. She recognised the black curls that clung to the nape of a man's neck beneath the green theatre cap and the strong cast of a man's handsome profile and the very slight drag of a man's long leg as he strode beside the patient.

She was astonished by the realisation that Griff Rydell had not only recovered remarkably well from his terrible injuries but had also resumed his promising career as a surgeon. They must have been close to encounter on several occasions that morning if he'd been one of the green-garbed figures she'd glimpsed through the round window of an operating room door or crossing the corridor or relaxing briefly with his colleagues in the surgeons' sitting-room between operations.

It seemed an ironic twist that he should be working at the very hospital in North Wales that had lured her from Marks Cross, and she couldn't help feeling that it really did seem that destiny had played some part in thrusting them in each other's way. Kelly didn't mind at all. But she felt that *he* would mind very much when he had time to realise her presence at the Porthbryn General. Passing her, he'd scarcely glanced in her direction, too concerned with the patient. But once he became aware that they would be working beneath the same roof and in the same department of the big hospital, he might resent the constant reminder of Kate and past unhappiness and might lump Kelly with her cousin as someone he no longer wished to know.

Just as he had on the previous day, she thought wryly.

She was about to turn away, due for her lunch-break, when the theatre sister appeared at the door of the ante-room and beckoned to her. 'Nurse Lorimer!'

Kelly hurried forward. 'Yes, Sister!'

'There's another accident case on its way so we shall have to use Number Two for this emergency. I hope it's ready for use?'

'Yes, quite ready, Sister.'

Angie nodded approval. 'Scrub for Mr Rydell, please. The patient has head and chest injuries so you'll need to lay up for a craniotomy and a thoracotomy. He's being stabilised at the moment but should be ready for surgery in fifteen minutes.'

'Very well, Sister.'

Angie hesitated. 'Sure you can cope? I'm sorry to thrust this in your lap on your first day but it can't be helped.'

'That's all right, Sister.'

'You'll miss your lunch, I'm afraid.'

Kelly smiled. 'It's an occupational hazard in theatre work, isn't it?' She hurried along the corridor to the gleaming theatre that stood in pristine and aseptic readiness for just such an emergency, and mustered her team for action. There was a lot to do at such short notice but the routine was so familiar that by the time the patient was trundled in and transferred from trolley to operating table, everything was ready for the surgeons.

Gowned and masked and gloved, fair hair tucked carefully inside the theatre cap, Kelly took sterile towels from the pack that was opened for her by Sharon and turned to drape them about the patient's already-shaved head.

As she sponged the operating area with aseptic solution, she mentally revised procedure with a little anxiety while she waited for Griff Rydell and his assistant surgeon who were scrubbing-up in the annexe.

He'd nodded to her as he entered the theatre and found her hard at work with the necessary preparations, but Kelly knew that it had been merely absent courtesy. He'd been so deep in discussion of the case with his colleague that he hadn't really looked at her, let alone recognised her, she thought dryly. Now, wearing a mask and with only her wide hazel eyes and delicately arched eyebrows showing, she doubted that he would recognise her even if he had the time or the inclination to wonder about the nurse who stood by to hand the instruments he needed or to swab for him.

The anaesthetist settled himself at the head of the unconscious patient and began to adjust taps and fiddle with tubing, casting a careful and responsible eye over the dials of his complicated equipment. The patient was wired to a monitor in case of cardiac difficulties and a respirator was assisting him with his breathing. He seemed to be in very poor shape.

Once he was satisfied that he had the patient's condition under control and that everything was working as it should, he took time off to glance at the busy scrub nurse.

'Hi! Aren't you the new nurse? The one with the glowing references?'

Kelly looked up. Her hazel eyes smiled at him above the mask. 'I don't know about the references but I *am* new. Kelly Lorimer,' she obliged.

'That's right,' he agreed, twinkling. 'Jeremy Hunt's gorgeous girlfriend. Welcome to Porthbryn General!'

'Thank you,' she said demurely, amused but not sure that she was pleased with the label she'd obviously acquired even before she set foot in Porthbryn.

He watched her thoughtfully as she went on with her preparations. 'How do you feel about being thrown in the deep end on your first day, Kelly?' It was a warm, friendly enquiry.

'Well, I don't intend to drown!'

He chuckled. 'Good girl,' he said, approving her spirit. 'You seem to know the ropes and you're lucky to have a good man for your first op. One of the best, in fact. Griff Rydell will see you through if you stumble and he won't bawl you out like some. Met him yet?'

'Not exactly . . .' It was only half a lie, she comforted herself, heart fluttering with trepidation as she wondered at the surgeon's reaction when he eventually realised the identity of the new scrub nurse.

'He's a Hartlake man so he's bound to welcome you with open arms,' the anaesthetist prophesied cheerfully. 'You're a clannish crowd. I'm John Duncan, by the way. I expect Jeremy's mentioned my name?'

'He's mentioned so many names . . .'

'Well, we're great mates so I know he won't mind if I take you out tonight to celebrate the birth of a beautiful friendship.' It was light-hearted, cheekily confident, and an infectious smile was reflected in the depths of his warm brown eyes.

Kelly had learned to judge character by the set and expression of eyes above a surgical mask and to assess sincerity by the way a smile dawned or danced or lingered in those eyes. John Duncan passed on both counts and she warmed to him instinctively.

'*I* might mind, however,' she protested lightly, not too discouraging, a smile in her own eyes. She bent over the patient to adjust the flow of the antibiotic that was being dripped into his vein via a cannula inserted in his arm. He looked grey and the respirator was doing most of his breathing for him. 'He's in a bad way,' she commented. 'What happened to him?'

'Head-on collision with another car, apparently. Two dead and three in critical condition, including this one. I'm not too happy about his chances, to be frank.'

'Just try to keep him alive while he's in my hands,

there's a good chap,' Griff Rydell said crisply, flexing strong hands in the thin surgical gloves as he approached, gowned and masked. He paused by the table, watching the scrub nurse's deft fingers as they worked, busy with the final preparations before surgery. Then he bent to examine the shaved and sterilised area of the man's head.

'That's a very nasty depression, isn't it?' He turned to his assistant, who'd followed him into the operating-room. 'I think we shall find subdural haematoma and extensive swelling of the brain, Richard.' He glanced at the anaesthetist, the most important member of the theatre team, for while the patient lay on the table his life depended on the man's skill and judgment and careful observation and prompt action. 'How is he now, John? Stable enough for us to begin operating?'

'He's under control at the moment, anyway. You can go ahead when you like.'

For the first time, the surgeon turned directly to the gowned and masked nurse who'd been making a last check of the array of gleaming instruments and now stood with a scalpel poised and ready to slap into his hand. 'Everything all right, Nurse? May we proceed?' he asked formally, following the rigid etiquette of the theatre.

'Certainly, Mr Rydell.'

Grey eyes narrowed and darkened. For a moment he looked into wide hazel orbs that stared back at him without flinching, although he'd caught the betraying tremor in her quiet voice as she said his name.

He'd heard snatches of conversation about the pretty new theatre nurse throughout the morning. Angie had told him that she would be scrubbing for this case and assured him that she was experienced and reliable. He couldn't recall that anyone had actually told him the girl's name. Now, he didn't need to wonder. He knew.

But he didn't say anything. He merely held out his hand for the scalpel . . .

CHAPTER THREE

WATCHING HIM work, Kelly was fascinated. He was a brilliant surgeon with an economy of movement and an unorthodox but highly effective technique that left her gasping with admiration. She had to work at full stretch to keep up with him, to anticipate his needs, to satisfy the unspoken but obvious demands of a perfectionist in his approach to surgery.

He was swift and sure, the strong hands cutting and clamping and clearing the debris of shattered bone and clotted blood and dead tissue to get to the source of the trouble. Having located it and relieved the pressure on the man's brain, he was satisfied that he'd operated in time to prevent severe and lasting damage. He checked pupil reaction and reflexes and then left his assistant to close and suture the head wound while he turned his attention to the chest injury.

He performed a thoracotomy that was a work of art, if not exactly text book in its procedure. Kelly was kept too busy to feel fatigued as she supplied instruments, swabbed, irrigated and held a receiver for the sections of rib that he had to remove from the patient's punctured lung.

He was working against time and the man's shocked condition. Suddenly a monitor bleeped a warning and Griff reached for a prepared hypodermic and shot the drug directly into the man's failing heart with scarcely a pause. The blip on the monitor faltered and stopped and everyone held their breath until it started again, picking up gradually until it resumed its regular and rhythmic beat. Then the surgeon returned to the chest cavity and the work of rib resection.

'I don't think he can take much more,' John warned quietly, several minutes later, scanning the monitors with some anxiety.

Griff straightened. 'I'm just about to close. There isn't anything more we can do but pray.' He'd been operating non-stop for nearly three hours. His eyes ached from concentration beneath the arc lights and his back ached, as it frequently did, from long standing, a legacy of the car crash of six years before.

'Perhaps you'd like to finish off, Richard.' He stepped back to watch while the slender scrub nurse checked the count of swabs and instruments before handing the needle-holder and sutures to his waiting assistant. 'Thank you, Nurse. You did very well,' he said abruptly and moved away from the table, his limp slightly more pronounced than before. He stripped off gown and gloves and mask to drop them in the dirty bin.

Kelly didn't even glance up in response to the curt words of praise. They were almost the first words he'd spoken to her directly, she thought wryly. They'd worked in such close harmony that he'd scarcely needed to ask for an instrument or issue an instruction throughout the entire proceedings. It would be fair to say she'd done remarkably well considering she was new to his style and methods, she thought wearily and without conceit. He could have spoken more warmly or tossed just one smile in her direction as a reward for her efforts.

There hadn't been the slightest flicker of recognition in those granite eyes throughout the last three hours of working together, but she was sure that he knew her identity well enough. He was just being bloody-minded—and she was too tired and too hungry to care.

When he left the operating room, it seemed to Kelly

that everyone visibly relaxed. She hadn't realised the
slight tension until that moment, too intent on doing
what was required of her to the best of her ability. Now,
she wondered if Griff Rydell was disliked or feared or if
he merely kept everyone on their toes with his de-
mandingly high standards. He was certainly dedicated to
surgery. But he had kept everyone at a distance while he
operated with that impersonal manner—and the
thought made her feel slightly less snubbed by his
unfriendly attitude.

'One of his bad days,' John said cryptically to the
junior registrar who'd taken the surgeon's place at the
operating table.

Richard Bowers nodded. 'He hates these accident
cases. Brings back the memories, I guess.' He glanced
up at Kelly. 'He was in a car accident some years ago. It
nearly put paid to his career as a surgeon, apparently.
He never speaks about it, of course. He isn't the type.
But he's super-charged with the determination to go flat
out to save this kind of patient . . . as you saw.'

'He seemed very intense,' she agreed carefully.

She said nothing about having known Griff before
that accident and its subsequent results. It might lead to
disclosures of a private kind that he would probably
resent. Pride had slammed the door on the past and she
felt that he didn't want it opened by her or anyone else.
It was understandable—but it left her firmly on the
outside, and that hurt for some inexplicable reason.

Richard was neat and methodical but painfully slow in
contrast to the senior registrar's swift and sure work.
However, at last the patient was wheeled away to the
intensive care unit and Kelly pulled off her mask and
looked about the theatre with a rueful expression. She
exchanged smiles with the two nurses who'd been so
responsible and supportive in the background.

'Help!' she said expressively.

With his mask dangling by its tapes, John was busy with the process of turning off taps, adjusting dials and shutting down cylinders of nitrous oxide and oxygen. 'That's called baptism by fire!' he said, the smile that lit his lean face just as engaging as the one she'd seen in his warm eyes whenever she'd looked his way.

'I'm feeling slightly scorched about the edges, I must admit.'

'You look very cool and collected.' The glow of admiration and the warm tone turned the light words into an unmistakable compliment.

Kelly smiled at him. Deep down, she wasn't thrilled about being labelled as Jeremy's girlfriend before she'd really made up her mind how she felt about him. She didn't feel ready to be tied too tightly to any man and she didn't want him talking and behaving as though they were virtually engaged. She was very fond of him but still a long way from loving, and she wanted to feel free to go out with other men if she wished. With this very personable anaesthetist, for instance, or other men she might meet while she worked at the Porthbryn General. Somehow, she must make that plain to Jeremy at her first opportunity—without hurting or disappointing him, of course.

Kelly didn't pause to wonder why her feelings had suddenly become so uncertain where he was concerned. Hadn't she come to Porthbryn to be with him, knowing how he would construe her decision and happy to let him think that their future lay together, with or without marriage? Hadn't she felt for months that he was the only man she would want to marry—one day, and if he asked her! Suddenly, hovering on the brink of commitment, something had made her hesitate, think again, doubt the depth of her feeling for him and his rightness for herself.

Kelly wasn't ready to analyse that *something* . . .

'You were marvellous,' Megan declared generously, bundling up the pile of used towels and sheets and thrusting them into the 'dirty' bin. 'I've never seen such team-work and he isn't the easiest of surgeons, according to Angie. She's always complaining about his unorthodox style. Were you reading the man's mind, or what!'

Kelly laughed. 'That would make life easy, if I could! No, it's just knowing procedure and being used to working with several different surgeons, I suppose. He threw me slightly at first but once I realised the way he went about things, it came easier.'

'He was very impressed. I heard him say so to Angie,' Sharon volunteered in her soft voice, looking up with her slightly shy smile from the tray of instruments she was preparing for the autoclave.

'Oh, this is embarrassing,' Kelly protested laughingly, warmth stealing into her face. 'I was only doing my job, you know!'

'And doing it very well, apparently.' As if she'd heard the sound of her name, the theatre sister walked into the operating room. She was smiling but Kelly fancied that little daggers of dislike lurked in the woman's dark eyes and she wondered if Angela Howell would have been better pleased if she hadn't coped so well with an unknown surgeon's style.

'You seem to have lived up to your splendid reputation, Nurse Lorimer.'

'I'm just glad that I didn't make any mistakes, Sister.' The surgeon might have overlooked them but the theatre sister would have been down on her like a ton of bricks, she thought dryly.

'Mr Rydell was very satisfied with the way you

scrubbed for him,' Angie swept on, a slight edge to the approval. 'He tells me that you are exceptionally well-trained and really know your surgery.'

'That was very kind of him. Thank you, Sister.' Kelly glowed with pride and warmed to the fairness that had prompted her senior to repeat the surgeon's words.

'He isn't the kind to criticise, of course,' Angie continued, spoiling the effect. 'He's a very tolerant surgeon, I've always found. So I knew he would make every allowance for your newness.'

'He had no cause for criticism and no need to make allowances,' John broke in promptly. 'No one could have faulted Kelly's work this afternoon, believe me! She's quick and efficient and she knew just what Griff was going to do before he did it—and that isn't easy, as you know for yourself, Angie! I swear she could have performed both operations herself if it had been necessary!'

Kelly's swift, sweet smile thanked the young anaesthetist but deplored the absurd exaggeration, and she wished that he hadn't leaped so hastily to her defence. His well-meaning support wasn't well-received by the woman who seemed to regard her as some kind of a rival, professionally and otherwise, she thought dryly.

'Your previous hospital must have been very sorry to lose you,' Angie commented, the smile just failing to reach her glittering dark eyes. 'I believe you were on the short list for promotion to theatre sister, too. It must be something very special that brought you all the way to Porthbryn!'

'I fancied a change, Sister.' Kelly didn't have the least inclination to satisfy the probing curiosity of the words.

'Their loss will be our gain if you keep up the good work.' Angie's glance swept the operating room, observing the efficient busyness of the staff nurses without obvious satisfaction. 'As soon as the theatre is ready for further use, you and your team may go off duty,' she went on briskly. 'You missed lunch, didn't you?'

Kelly nodded. 'Thank you, Sister.'

About to turn away, Angie paused. 'There are three cases on tomorrow's list for this theatre, Nurse Lorimer. All routine. A tonsillectomy, a hernia and a cholecystectomy. They won't present any problems for you, obviously. I dare say you can deal with them all yourself if we happen to be short of surgeons!' It was slightly sardonic banter, thinly veiling the hostility.

Kelly smiled dutifully and resisted the childish impulse to thumb her nose at the departing theatre sister's back.

John looked at her curiously. 'She seems to have taken a dislike to you,' he said shrewdly. 'What did you do to upset our Angie on your very first day, I wonder?'

Everyone spoke of her almost affectionately, Kelly had noticed. So it must be only herself who brought out the worst in Angela Howell's nature, she thought ruefully.

'I think she's just rushed,' she said lightly. 'It's an awful lot of responsibility for one pair of shoulders.'

But although she shrugged off the suggestion of malice, she knew it had been present in the woman's attitude and it didn't escape her notice that Megan and Sharon exchanged meaningful glances and stayed silent.

Kelly was all the more convinced that everyone but herself knew that Jeremy and Angela Howell had been rather more than professionally involved in recent weeks—and no doubt everyone was waiting to see what would happen now that 'Jeremy's girlfriend' had arrived on the scene!

John went on with the task of shutting down his equipment and Kelly was much too busy to talk to the anaesthetist as she helped the other nurses with the cleaning of the theatre. But he managed to have a quiet word with her before he went away to change.

'I know we've only just met, and I don't want to rush you into anything—and I'm not sure how things are with you and Jeremy. But I'd like to take you out one night, Kelly. What are my chances?' he asked directly.

She liked the straightforward approach and the obvious sincerity. She liked him, too.

'I'm not sure how things are with me and Jeremy, either,' she admitted frankly, thinking of her own inexplicable doubts as well as the possibility that Angela Howell had some claim on his affection and attention these days. 'But I don't think that's a bar to friendship with other people. Give me a few days to settle in and perhaps we can arrange to meet one evening for a drink or a meal or something.' It wasn't exactly a promise but it was encouragement and she saw the glow of satisfaction in his warm brown eyes.

'I'm only one of a number of anaesthetists on the staff, obviously. So it might be some days before you see me in Number Two Theatre. But wild horses won't keep me from seeing you in the meantime,' he promised lightly.

Kelly laughed and looked after him with liking, not really sure that he was serious, not really sure that she wanted him to be. For the moment, Jeremy was sufficient complication in her life. But if he should fail her . . .

As soon as the work was done, she sent Megan and Sharon off duty. Then she stood in the empty operating room and surveyed it critically, assuring herself for perhaps the eighth time that it was spick and span and as sterile as it could be. She was possibly too conscious of her new responsibilities and the feeling that Angela

Howell was just waiting for her to put a foot wrong, she thought ruefully. She might be just a little too concerned with impressing a certain surgeon with her abilities, too, she admitted, suddenly impatient with herself for caring what Griff Rydell thought or felt about her.

Emerging from the theatre, she met Jeremy in the corridor. He'd been operating all the afternoon but he'd snatched a few moments between cases to look in on a fellow surgeon's work. Before slipping away again, he'd given Kelly a smile and the thumbs-up sign in silent approval and encouragement.

Now he greeted her with a very special smile. 'How's my girl?' he asked lightly. 'You *have* had a busy first day, haven't you?'

'It's been hectic,' she agreed.

'And you've loved every minute of it.' His eyes were warm with affection and understanding.

Her heart smote her as she realised that she'd not only doubted his continued feeling for her but almost hoped that it had been replaced by an affection for someone else—even if she couldn't like that someone else at all!

'Yes, I have enjoyed it. I'm sorry I missed our lunch date, though.'

'A sandwich and a cup of doubtful coffee from the staff cafeteria? Not much of a miss.' With a weary gesture he pulled off his theatre cap and ran a hand through red-gold hair that was damp-darkened by sweat. The faint and slightly sickly smell of ether clung to him, but Kelly was too used to that to notice. It clung to her, too—hair and skin and clothes. A shower and a shampoo were the first essentials for every surgeon and nurse after working in Theatres.

'We'll have dinner this evening instead,' Jeremy suggested. 'All right?'

Kelly looked doubtful. He'd been on call the previous

night and operating all day. 'Aren't you tired?' she protested in instant concern.

'Sure I'm tired,' he said with just a hint of impatience as if he suspected her of reluctance. 'But we haven't seen much of each other lately, Kelly. I've missed you.'

'Yes, I know.' She hesitated, discovering to her dismay that she *was* reluctant—and that was absurd when she'd known him so long and so well and was so fond of him and had felt in recent weeks that her life was rather empty without him. What on earth was happening to her! Hadn't she come to Porthbryn to be with him whenever she could? She smiled at him, quick and warm. 'I've missed you, too,' she said with truth. 'Where shall we meet? The Flying Horse? It's only a step for you and only a few minutes in the car for me.'

With time and place agreed, they separated and Jeremy went back to the theatre to carry on operating, his list unfinished due to the emergency cases. As she turned away, Kelly saw that Angela Howell stood at the open door of her office. She'd obviously been watching and listening to that brief exchange. *If looks could kill*, Kelly thought, taken aback by the venom in those glittering dark eyes.

Standing under the shower, long hair streaming and newly-washed and scented by her favourite shampoo, Kelly wondered if light-hearted Jeremy had been stringing the theatre sister along without really meaning to do so. He didn't exactly flirt but he didn't have the heart to snub, either, she thought ruefully, remembering other girls who'd fancied him and attached too much importance to the way he looked and smiled and spoke when it was just Jeremy being Jeremy. He was everyone's friend, good-natured and obliging and eager to please. The warm generosity and easy friendliness could be very misleading, she knew.

It had been a long time before level-headed Kelly had allowed herself to like him too much or take him too seriously. Then, she had believed that she was just one more of the many harmless flirtations in his life. Now, she accepted that she was important to him and that he wanted a permanent relationship, even if marriage hadn't been mentioned. She had yet to make up her mind how important he was to her—and how much it would matter if he never mentioned marriage. Kelly was proud and rather independent and old-fashioned enough to still be a virgin, and she was reluctant to give a great deal for a doubtful return.

She was much too modest to suppose that every man she met was likely to fall in love with her, too. But Angela Howell might be cast in a different mould. Kelly couldn't like the woman but she didn't want anyone to be hurt by an unsuspecting and well-meaning Jeremy. She wondered if it might be a good idea to drop a gentle hint in his ear . . .

Kelly arrived early at the pub where she'd arranged to meet Jeremy that evening. The Flying Horse was a favourite with the staff of the Porthbryn General for its convenient locality as well as the warm and friendly atmosphere that turned it into a club rather than pub. It was a pleasant and peaceful place with timbered ceiling and walls, rather dated decor and lighting and no space invader machines or juke boxes to attract a rougher element.

Entering, she hesitated and almost turned tail at sight of the tall man who was talking to the publican at the bar. But she stood her ground, heart bumping in her breast for absolutely no good reason. Formally dressed in a dark-blue suit, laughing in response to some remark of the publican's, he was handsome and impressive and much more attractive than any man ought to be, Kelly decided with an unwelcome shock of response to Griff Rydell's physical magnetism, even at that distance.

Griff turned his head when the publican drew his attention to the girl who stood just inside the door, hesitant, looking his way. His glance swept her from head to toe without apparent interest, but it took in the loveliness of long pale hair framing a heart-shaped face and the near-fragility of a slender figure in a soft pink dress that seemed to reflect some of its delicate colour into her cheeks.

She looked very pretty and absurdly youthful and not at all like the impersonal scrub nurse who'd inspired his reluctant admiration for her expertise and efficiency that afternoon. Now, he felt an equally reluctant admiration for the girl herself, but it didn't dispel his resentment at her link with a past that he was trying to forget. She stirred too many painful memories.

Kelly looked back at him, more challenging than she knew with that slight tilt to her chin and her hazel eyes sparking with a hint of defiance. Then she began to walk towards the bar where he stood. Griff turned back to the publican and resumed their conversation so pointedly that it was a rebuff. She pretended not to realise it, determined that he shouldn't brush her off as a nuisance and a nothing this time. Maybe he *didn't* want to know her but it was unavoidable since destiny had decreed that they should work together at the Porthbryn General Hospital.

Reaching him, she touched him lightly on the arm in friendly fashion. 'Hi . . .'

She felt him stiffen. Then he looked at her and inclined that proud, dark head in the merest nod of acknowledgment and put out a hand to pick up his drink. The colour rushed into her face at an obvious put-down.

'Evening, miss . .' The publican was friendlier,

smiling a welcome, remembering her from a previous occasion when she'd been accompanied by Jeremy. 'Miss Lorimer, isn't it? I've a message for you from Mr Hunt. He just telephoned to say that he's been delayed at the hospital and hopes you won't mind waiting.'

Kelly nodded, unsurprised. 'Thank you.'

'He said you were to order anything you liked and he'd settle with me later. So what can I get for you, miss?'

'Martini and lemonade, please.' As the man turned to the optics, she tried once more with the silent surgeon at her side. 'That's the drawback to dating doctors. Their work so often gets in the way of their social life,' she said lightly, inviting agreement rather than sympathy. He made no answer, studying the level of the lager in his tall glass before raising it to his lips. Kelly suddenly lost patience. 'I wish you'd stop behaving as though you don't know me!' she said sharply. 'It's so *silly!*'

He raised a cool eyebrow. 'But I *don't* know you,' he drawled. 'We met once or twice some years ago and exchanged perhaps half a dozen words. Any intimacy between us existed solely in your mind, I'm afraid.'

'Well, that's blunt!' she said, quick and indignantly.

Griff shrugged. 'Take offence if you wish. I came in here for a quiet drink and I'm in no mood to rake over the past with you or anyone else,' he said, even more bluntly.

'Sorry I spoke!' she said, tartly. She took her drink from the publican with a slightly forced smile and moved away to a quiet corner table, seething.

Hateful, despicable man!

Heaven knew why she'd bothered to speak to him when he'd made it so plain that their only relationship was an enforced professional one that stopped at the swing doors of Theatres . . .

CHAPTER FOUR

'The lady looks upset . . .' The publican jerked his head in the direction of the slender girl who sat so stiffly in a chair, revolving the untouched Martini between her fingers, eyes fixed on the door in slightly anxious vigil.

Griff didn't turn to look at her as the man obviously expected. 'Women don't like to be kept waiting, do they?' he said carelessly, indifferent.

'She's a pretty girl. Lovely smile. The boyfriend wants to watch he doesn't lose her, turning up late for dates. I could fancy her myself if the wife wasn't watching!' Bob Crane chuckled. 'Nurse, is she? It isn't such a bad life for you doctors, is it? All those good-looking young nurses and loads of opportunity!'

As the big man moved away to serve another customer, Griff looked up from his lager to study Kelly Lorimer's reflection in the mirror behind the bar. Her eyes were very bright and her face slightly flushed. He wondered why she was so persistent in trying to establish a friendly relationship between them—and if he'd been a trifle unkind. She was a pretty girl with considerable appeal for a sensual man like himself, but that smile had a disturbing quality with its forceful reminder of Kate.

Abruptly, he picked up his lager and crossed the room to her corner. He sat down without invitation or approval and placed his drink on the table between them.

'Sorry,' he said brusquely, unsmiling. 'That was unforgivably rude.'

It wasn't much of an apology and Kelly looked at him coldly. 'Then you can't expect to be forgiven.'

'I don't. I'm not particularly interested in what you think about me.'

'Then why bother to apologise?'

'I'm damned if I know, except that you were looking rather crushed.'

'You meant to crush me!'

'Perhaps I did.' A smile flickered briefly in the grey eyes. He regarded her thoughtfully. 'What the devil brought you to Porthbryn?'

She almost told him that she'd wanted to be near Jeremy. Instead, she shrugged. 'One of those things . . .'

He nodded. 'We need you, of course. You're a bloody good nurse.'

Kelly was surprised into a smile by the obvious sincerity of the vehement words. 'Nice of you to say so.'

'It wasn't meant as a compliment,' he said dryly. 'Mere statement of fact. Trained at Hartlake, did you? You weren't a nurse when I knew you.'

'You never knew me,' she reminded him.

Griff laughed. '*Touché!*'

He was a different man when he laughed like that, Kelly thought impulsively; so warm and human and likeable, so dangerously attractive, too. For her heart fluttered quite foolishly in response to the twin candles of humour that glowed in the grey eyes.

Unaccountably flustered, she rushed into speech. 'I began my training some months after . . .' She broke off abruptly, biting her lip, realising where the words were leading her. She'd felt they were suddenly near to making real contact. Now, she'd probably driven him further away with that tactless reminder.

'After my accident,' he finished in level tones.

She nodded. 'Yes.'

'You may mention it,' he told her dryly. 'I won't bite your head off.'

'To see you now, looking so fit and back in a job that you obviously love and certainly do well . . .' She smiled at him suddenly. 'It hardly seems possible and I'm so happy for you, Griff.'

He side-stepped the emotional stir of those heartfelt words. 'Yes, well, there's no need to mention it to Kate if you're in touch with her these days,' he said brusquely.

Kelly hesitated. 'I think she'd want to know,' she said quietly.

'To ease her conscience, I dare say.'

'She did care.'

'Not enough,' he interrupted harshly. 'Let's not discuss it. I'll get you another drink.'

Kelly divided her attention between watching the door for Jeremy and watching the surgeon who stood at the bar with his back to her. She could understand the way he felt about Kate but she thought he was wrong to leave her cousin with a burden of guilt. He'd rebuilt his health and his career and got on with his life without Kate by his side. Surely it would relieve her cousin's mind to know that she hadn't destroyed him utterly with that desertion at the worst possible time in a man's life. Kelly felt that *she* would want to know, in similar circumstances.

Griff came back with the drinks, sat down. 'Tell me about Kate. Is she happy?' he demanded abruptly.

Kelly wasn't sure what he hoped to hear but she could only tell him the truth. 'I believe she's very happy,' she said quietly.

He nodded. 'Children?'

'Two little girls. Emma's three. Josephine is just four months.' She thought she saw him wince and her heart ached for the man who'd loved Kate, planned to marry her, hoped for children to bond their loving relationship.

'What was he . . . the man she married? Engineer of sorts?'

'Managing director of an engineering firm in Peterborough.'

'So she can't want for anything. Good. One likes to know these things,' he said, matter of factly. 'Now that's out of the way we needn't mention Kate again.'

Kelly leaned to touch his hand in a small gesture of compassion. 'I'm sorry, Griff,' she said gently.

He jerked from that well-meaning touch. 'Save your sympathy for those who need it,' he drawled. 'Kate did me a favour. I might still be in that wheelchair if she hadn't backed out of marrying me. I set out to prove that I wasn't the total wreck that she thought. And I did it, by God!'

'It can't have been easy.'

He looked at her for a long moment. 'No. But it was worth all the effort. And I've no regrets. None at all. So you can stop regarding me with those sorrowful eyes and mourning for my might-have-been. As far as I'm concerned, it's the never-meant-to-be and belongs to the past. Let's just leave it there.'

She didn't believe him. She felt that he was still very much in love with Kate. She felt that he was a lonely and saddened man who'd dedicated his life to surgery because he thought there was nothing else left to him. Her tender heart went out to him and she wished there was some way that she could make up for the heartache and disappointment that her spoiled and selfish cousin had caused him.

'I'm sorry I had to dredge it all up again,' she said quietly, ruefully.

Griff shrugged. 'Don't worry your pretty head about

it,' he said. 'All I ask is that you get on with the job that you came here to do and don't try to trade on past acquaintance. You and I have nothing in common.'

It was just as though he'd read her mind. Kelly's face flamed. 'I hope you don't think that I'm interested in you!' she said defensively. 'You're just the man that my cousin nearly married, that's all—and if you were as insufferable in those days as you are now then I'm not surprised that she couldn't go through with it!'

She leaped to her feet and hurried to meet Jeremy, just arriving, feeling that she'd never been quite so pleased to see anyone. She greeted him much more warmly than was probably wise considering that her feelings were so unsettled where he was concerned. But it didn't seem to matter too much that he might get the wrong impression as long as Griff Rydell realised that she had neither the need nor the desire to run after him. She was perfectly happy with Jeremy, who not only cared for her but wouldn't dream of saying such brutally blunt things to her!

She urged him out of the place on the pretext that it was much too nice an evening to be spent in a stuffy pub. 'Why don't we drive to the sea front and stroll along the promenade and then have a drink at one of those pubs with the outside tables before we have dinner?' she suggested brightly.

'Just as you like,' Jeremy agreed easily. 'We'll take my car and leave yours here for the time being, I think. It'll be quite safe.'

'Who'd want it?' she retorted lightly. But she gave the Mini an affectionate pat on the bonnet in passing in case it took offence and refused to start when she came back for it later that night.

Jeremy settled her beside him and kissed her briefly

before turning on the ignition. She smiled at him, determined that the rankling remarks of another man shouldn't spoil the evening for either of them.

'Sorry I was late, love. I had a mastoidectomy listed for tomorrow morning but the poor kid was in so much pain that I felt I ought to do it right away.'

'I guessed it was something like that. And you weren't so very late.'

'You appeared to be in good hands, anyway,' he said lightly, manoeuvring the car into the stream of traffic on the busy road that led to the town and the sea front. 'Griff was late leaving the hospital, too. He was rather concerned about that patient in ICU. But I dare say he told you.'

'We were just chatting. We didn't talk shop.' It was evasive, although she didn't suspect good-natured Jeremy of probing.

'He said some very nice things about you this afternoon, you know. Then I find him chatting you up while my back is turned. Does he fancy you? Should I be jealous?'

His glancing smile and the twinkle in the blue eyes implied a confidence in her love and loyalty that made Kelly feel strangely uncomfortable.

'Heavens no!' she exclaimed brightly. 'He doesn't say nice things to me, I assure you. He was just being polite . . . with an effort. I get the impression that he doesn't like me at all—and the feeling happens to be mutual!' It wasn't strictly true, but she preferred not to dwell on the inexplicable tug of attraction for a man who meant to keep her firmly at a distance.

Jeremy looked at her in some surprise. 'Really? You're the only person I know who doesn't like him, Kelly.'

She shrugged. 'That should be good for him. No one

should be one hundred per cent popular or they soon become one hundred per cent conceit.'

'He's a fantastic surgeon,' he said generously.

'That doesn't necessarily make him my kind of person. I admire his work. I just don't like his style,' she said airily. 'Must we talk about him? Can't we talk about something more interesting?' Eventually Jeremy would discover that she'd met Griff Rydell some years earlier but she didn't feel that she had the right to disclose the surgeon's secrets.

'Us, for instance?' he said promptly, predictably.

'Why not?' she agreed recklessly.

'You, anyway.' He reached for her hand and took it to his lips in a lover's gesture, but Kelly had the oddest feeling that he'd hedged. 'It's great to have you here at last, love.'

'I'm happy to be here.' Even as she spoke, she felt that her tone lacked conviction. But it was absurd to feel that all her pleasure in the new job had suddenly evaporated because a man who didn't really matter had said some hurtful things.

'We're going to have a lot of fun,' Jeremy promised warmly.

'Well, I hope so . . .'

But her heart sank slightly. Fun? Was it all no more than a game to Jeremy and would it never be anything else for all his talk of loving her, needing her? No wonder she felt so reluctant to commit herself too finally to their relationship, she thought wryly. She had to feel secure in a man's love and his promises for the future. Maybe she was ridiculously old-fashioned, but she needed to feel that a man loved her enough to want to marry her, to make that commitment to her in private and before the world, before she could give without counting the cost . . .

He took her to a nightclub where the food and the wine were very good and a well-known comedian was the star of the cabaret. Kelly did her best to enjoy the evening but somehow it wasn't the success that it should have been. Jeremy was attentive and amusing and very affectionate—and all with an effort, she sensed, wondering if the few months that he'd spent in Porthbryn without her had altered his feeling for her and strained their easy relationship.

He was tired, she knew. But he didn't seem to be relaxed or entirely comfortable in her company and she wondered if he was also haunted by the thought of someone else that evening.

Was he torn between a sense of obligation towards the girl he'd persuaded to come to Porthbryn and a growing attachment to another girl? Had he fallen out of love with her and into love with the very attractive theatre sister at the Porthbryn General—and didn't have the heart to tell her so until she'd found her feet in the new job? If so, she could imagine that Angela Howell was giving him a bad time and she wondered if he'd kept their date that evening in the face of the girl's disapproval.

It was just the kind of situation that someone as kind-hearted and easy-going as Jeremy would get himself into, she thought wryly. It wouldn't be the end of the world if she was right, of course. But it would be a blow. He meant a lot to her or she'd never have come to Porthbryn with the possibility of marrying him in mind—and she wasn't prepared to hand him over without protest to a girl she didn't even like!

'Whatever are you thinking about, Kelly? You look positively militant,' Jeremy teased, smiling at her across the table.

'Do I?' She laughed. Then she said with the impulsiveness that so often led her astray, 'I was just thinking how nice you are and how I'd hate to lose you.' Words and smile were very warm and so was the look in her hazel eyes.

He met it without flinching. 'What makes you think I'm so easily lost? I won't slip through your fingers unless you choose to let go, love.'

It was the reassurance that she had deliberately invited but perversely it wasn't welcome. She'd given him an opening to tell her about Angie and he hadn't taken it, so it seemed that she must be mistaken about that sensed involvement with the theatre sister. She ought to be relieved and thankful that he still loved her, still wanted her. So why did she suddenly feel that she was falling into a trap of her own making?

She backed away from the hint of intensity in his blue eyes. 'Oh, I'll hold on to you until something better comes along,' she said brightly, bantering.

He followed her lead. 'Then I'll be around for a very long time, Kelly. For you won't find better than me,' he told her with smiling confidence.

He was teasing but she was abruptly serious. 'That's true,' she said, meaning it. For Jeremy had all the qualities that most women would look for in a man, she felt. His only fault was that odd reluctance to mention marriage—and that was the real bar to any change in their present relationship as far as Kelly was concerned.

With an engagement ring on her finger and a date set for the wedding, she felt that she could give herself wholeheartedly to loving. But without that promise of total commitment on Jeremy's part she wasn't ready to trust him with her heart. Or anything else.

So she had no hesitation in refusing when he asked her to stay with him at the flat instead of going back to the caravan that night.

Coffee cooling in the cups, he held her close, no longer trying to persuade her with kisses and caresses but needing her nearness while he struggled with his disappointment and his longing. Kelly lay in his arms on the deep-cushioned sofa in the sitting-room of his flat and wished she loved him enough to be generous.

He'd taken her refusal with a good grace, as always. But she still felt guilty. Not because she continued to say no to him but because she was never tempted to say yes, if the truth was told, she admitted wryly. His kiss was pleasant but unexciting; his touch left her unaroused and she simply couldn't pretend to want him when she didn't.

The vital spark had always been missing in her feeling for Jeremy but she'd comforted herself in the past with the thought that love, when it eventually came, would trigger desire and she'd be just as responsive as he could wish. Now, she was shaken to realise that love wasn't an essential ingredient for sexual yearning. She'd been stirred by an unaccountable and unwelcome but unmistakable ache of longing for the ardent lovemaking of a man she scarcely knew.

It was frightening to realise that she might be very tempted to melt into Griff Rydell's exciting embrace without a moment's hesitation if he should ever reach out for her. He never would, of course. Kelly hardly knew whether to be glad or sorry about that . . .

Jeremy drove her to the Flying Horse to pick up her car. It was very late. The pub was dark and deserted at that hour, of course, and the Mini was the only car on the forecourt, looking shabby and forlorn in the light of the street lamps.

Jeremy didn't immediately lean across to open the car door for her to get out. 'I hate all this,' he declared vehemently. 'It's such a hare-brained idea, sleeping alone in a caravan in the middle of a field miles from anywhere—and dangerous, too. There are all sorts of doubtful characters in these parts during the summer season, you know. I wish you'd move in with me, Kelly. We'll live like brother and sister if that's the way you want it, but at least let me look after you!'

She leaned against him and put her hand to his cheek in a little gesture of gratitude and affection. 'I might take you up on that suggestion after a few weeks of the caravan. But let me try it first—and please don't worry about me. I can take care of myself, you know.'

He sighed, captured her hand in his own and held it firmly. 'I can't help worrying about you. I feel so responsible. If it wasn't for me you wouldn't have come to Porthbryn!'

'No one can blame you for the caravan. That was entirely my idea.'

'You didn't want to know my idea,' he reminded her, a little wearily. 'But it was a much better one, you know.'

She smiled. 'I'm an old-fashioned girl. I just didn't fancy living in sin,' she said lightly.

'Sin! My God, you *are* old-fashioned!'

It was so impatient that Kelly was startled. She realised that she'd offended him with the light words and she decided not to add that she wouldn't consider it a sin if she loved him.

'Perhaps you ought to look for a girl with a more modern outlook,' she suggested gently.

'Perhaps I will.' He instantly regretted the swift retort. He put out a hand to twine his fingers in the pale strands of her long hair. 'Oh, Kelly,' he sighed. 'Don't make me say things to hurt you. You know you're the only girl I want . . .'

Kelly was glad to scramble behind the wheel of her

car and head for home. It had been a full and oddly emotional, draining day and she was very tired.

The caravan did seem lonely as she carefully picked her way across the field by the light of a powerful torch. The moon had been out earlier, full and mellow, but now it seemed to be hiding behind a bank of cloud. She refused to remember what Jeremy had said about doubtful characters.

Safely inside, she secured the door firmly and was soon between the sheets of her narrow bunk bed. But it was some time before she slept, for her thoughts seemed to be a confused jumble of the day in Theatres, the unsatisfactory encounters with the disturbingly attractive Griff Rydell and the evening she'd spent with the man who was asking more of her than she might ever be able to give . . .

Kelly woke with a start and a thumping heart and lay rigid with fear. Someone was trying to break down the door of the flimsy caravan and she was alone—quite unprotected and no match for a determined intruder!

Then the awareness of daylight filtering in at the windows and a plaintive bellow told her that it was merely one of the cows who'd blundered into the side of the van, and she breathed again.

But she was annoyed with herself for giving way to such a foolish attack of nerves as she waited for her heart to quieten and her pulses to slow down. It was all Jeremy's fault for filling her head with quite unnecessary anxieties so that she'd give up the caravan, she thought crossly, rolling over to look at the time.

The cow had acted as a timely alarm clock, she realised, throwing back the sheets and leaping out of bed to bustle about the tiny caravan before leaving for the hospital. She was due on duty at eight and with a busy morning ahead of her, she couldn't afford to be late—

she didn't want to give Angela Howell the least cause to complain about her time-keeping or anything else.

She drove through the gates of the hospital behind a dark blue and very distinctive car that stopped to drop a passenger by the main entrance. Driving past on her way to the car park, Kelly noticed that the slender and striking brunette bestowed a particularly enchanting smile on the man behind the wheel before she turned towards the building.

She'd recognised both car and driver instantly and she felt a foolish clutch of dismay at her heart. Perhaps she'd had it all wrong from the beginning. Maybe it was Griff and not Jeremy who was involved with the attractive Angela Howell. Had he told her about that chance meeting with a girl he'd once known? And told it in such a way that the theatre sister was bound to regard her with cold and suspicious eyes when she turned up at the Porthbryn General? Did she think that Kelly had taken the job of scrub nurse at this particular hospital just to be near Griff? He didn't have the slightest interest in her, but a jealous woman might think otherwise—and a jealous woman could be much more dangerous than a very attractive man . . .

CHAPTER FIVE

BY THE time that Kelly had found somewhere to park, being much too lowly to merit a reserved bay, made her way through a maze of hospital departments and corridors to Main Hall and the lifts, carefully avoiding the surgeon who was deep in conversation with a ward sister, and ascended to the top floor, she was almost late.

She pushed through the swing doors of Theatres to find that Angela Howell had already changed into green cotton dress and covered her gleaming dark hair with the regulation mob cap and was talking to the night sister who she was in the process of relieving from duty.

'. . . super time, thanks. A night out with a very eligible bachelor was just what I needed after a day like yesterday. Tall, dark and handsome is just my type, too,' she declared, the words carrying clearly along the corridor. She looked just like a cat which had been at the cream in Kelly's admittedly prejudiced view.

Angie turned as she approached and almost had a smile for her on the strength of that obviously enjoyable evening. 'Good morning, Nurse Lorimer.' She glanced at the wall clock. 'You're exactly on time, I see. You seem to possess all the virtues.'

'Good morning, Sister.' Kelly was formal, finding it quite impossible to smile, even if she could believe that it was only light-hearted and kindly-meant banter. She felt such a surge of totally incomprehensible dislike for a fellow nurse that she was shocked at herself.

She had absolutely no proof that the theatre sister had spent the previous evening with tall, dark and handsome

Griff Rydell, she told herself firmly. And the girl's arrival in his car early that morning didn't have to mean that they'd spent the night together—and it was none of her business if they had, anyway. She didn't care what he did or who he did it with, so she had no good reason to feel like slapping that slightly superior smile from Angela Howell's attractive face.

'I don't think you've met Sister Keith? She's in charge of Theatres at night and you'll be working with her on occasions, of course. Sister, this is our new paragon, Nurse Lorimer. Everyone's singing her praises, as I dare say you've heard.' There was just the hint of an edge to the words.

Mary Keith had smiling eyes and a sweet set to her mouth and there was real warmth in the shake of her hand. 'Kelly, isn't it?' she said gently. 'I'm sure that's the name I've heard so much lately on the lips of a surgeon who shall be nameless.'

Kelly laughed. 'I think you must mean Jeremy Hunt.'

'Yes, I think I do,' she agreed, twinkling. 'I gather that you're old friends.'

'We worked together at Marks Cross before he came here.'

'So he told me. I gather that he used all his powers of persuasion to get you to follow him to Porthbryn?' There was indulgence for a pair of lovers in the way that Mary spoke and smiled.

'Oh, he can be very persuasive,' Kelly said lightly.

'You haven't forgotten that you're responsible for your theatre being ready for use this morning, I suppose, Nurse Lorimer?' Angie broke in rather sharply. 'There are three operations on the list for your theatre and you have an early start, you know.'

It was unmistakable reproof for lingering to talk when she ought to be changing—and all because her friendship with Jeremy was the subject under discussion, Kelly thought shrewdly. She wondered if the theatre sister had a possessive hand on each of two surgeons—and which one she really wanted!

'Yes, I do know, Sister. But I left it in perfect order before I went off duty yesterday,' she said with a touch of spirit.

Angie frowned at her tone. 'But you don't know that it hasn't been used for an emergency in the meantime,' she pointed out, tartly. 'It may not be in perfect order at the moment. You have a hernia repair listed for nine and Mr Fleming likes to have everything ready for him when he arrives. He's fussy and very slow and I expect you'll find him a trial after assisting one of our star surgeons yesterday. But as it isn't one of Mr Rydell's operating days, I'm afraid you'll have to settle for working with lesser mortals.'

As she'd cherished neither the hope nor the expectation of scrubbing for Griff, and didn't have the least wish to see or speak to him, it seemed unlikely that it was disappointment that stirred in Kelly's breast at the words. Probably a touch of indigestion after a rushed breakfast, she told herself firmly.

'Oh, I've worked with all kinds, Sister,' she said with a coolly confident smile that was calculated to irritate. She could play an offensive game, too, if that was what Angie Howell wanted!

'We have a Kardex on each of our surgeons to list their pet hates and so on. Don't hesitate to refer to it if you're in any doubt at all about anything. Even a Hartlake nurse has the occasional doubt, I dare say,' Angie said dryly and with some malice.

'Jeremy mentioned that you trained at Hartlake,' Mary interposed, as if she was unaware of the tension between the two girls and its cause. 'I wonder if you knew Griff Rydell in the days when he worked there? We all feel that there must be some mystery about those days for he never talks about them at all, you know. Except to say that he had a bad car accident and had to give up surgery for a few years.'

Kelly supposed that any man as attractive as Griff Rydell must excite curiosity and speculation among the nurses at the Porthbryn General—particularly as he was also a very eligible bachelor. 'That was before my time,' she said carefully and with perfect truth.

'So you never knew him? How disappointing!'

Kelly didn't contradict the night sister's light words. Smiling, she hurried away to change her clothes for the day's work.

It was very routine that day, and the next, and she realised just how much she'd enjoyed working with a surgeon who'd challenged her efficiency and expertise at every turn. In a way, she was already spoiled for working with any of the other competent surgeons at the Porthbryn General, she thought wryly, cleaning and tidying the theatre after another tonsillectomy performed by slow and punctilious and very irritating Henry Fleming. At the same time, it was much more restful on the nerves—and her emotions.

Kelly knew that she'd been prompted by pride to prove her worth as a scrub nurse to a man who obviously didn't value her as a person in her own right. She wished that she could have taken pleasure in his approval instead of feeling so foolishly hurt by Griff Rydell's determined dismissal of any claim she might feel she had to his notice or his friendship.

It hadn't been fair or true to accuse her of trying to build a casual acquaintance and a few encounters into a near-romance, even if he had known of her youthful fancy for him at the time, and she was still smarting from the implication. For they hadn't been complete strangers, either, she thought defensively. But he'd made it plain that he wasn't interested in knowing her now and she was happy to follow his lead, she told herself firmly.

He'd been operating in Number Four Theatre that morning but he'd made no effort to see or speak to her and Kelly told herself proudly that it didn't matter in the least and it was no more than she expected after the words she'd thrown at him at their last encounter.

She knew that he'd left Theatres when his list was finished but she still found herself looking swiftly and almost expectantly at every man in surgical greens who crossed her path that afternoon. She was feeling rather cross with herself for it by the time she was due to go off duty and so she resolutely didn't glance up into the face of the man in green tunic and trousers who collided with her as she hurried to the changing-room. She kept her gaze firmly fixed on a spot somewhere in the middle of his chest and murmured an automatic apology.

'You look shell-shocked. Has it been that kind of day?' Griff drawled, steadying her with a strong hand.

Kelly looked up quickly and found cool, ironic amusement in the grey eyes. She wondered with a little leap of her heart if he could possibly know just how foolishly pleased she was to see him and how she had reacted to his touch.

'Oh! It's you!' she exclaimed, even more foolishly, a betraying warmth stealing into her face. 'I'm so sorry. I've a bad habit of cutting corners, I'm afraid.'

He regarded her with a lift to a dark eyebrow, observing the flush and the fluster and interpreting them correctly. 'Fortunately, you can do less damage to me than you did to my car,' he told her dryly. But even as he spoke, he wondered if those hazel eyes with their very expressive depths might not have the power to do a great deal of damage to a man's resolve if he allowed it to happen.

There was something about her that attracted him strongly. A physical likeness to Kate, perhaps, or the proud spirit that was entirely her own or simply the very disturbing appeal of her enchanting femininity. But one Lorimer was enough in any man's life, he told himself firmly. He had no intention of getting involved with another, even if she *was* all invitation and warm encouragement in the way she looked and smiled.

Griff knew that women found him attractive. He could scarcely not know, and sometimes he took advantage of a woman's interest. But he never allowed any woman to get really close to him, to penetrate the armour he'd wrapped about himself since the car crash that had cost him so much he held dear . . . the woman he wanted to marry, the hope of a surgical consultancy, the active outdoor life he'd enjoyed and so many friends.

Kate had walked away from him. His career had been broken off at the worst possible moment for an ambitious surgeon. Golf and tennis and running had been abruptly curtailed and friends had dropped away one by one as his life followed a different path via a number of operations, long sojourns in various hospitals and a determined course of physiotherapy to enable him to walk and work again.

'You were unexpected,' Kelly said lamely.

'Running into me is an occupational hazard for theatre nurses as I seem to spend most of my life in this place,' he returned smoothly.

She instantly felt that the mockery in his eyes and the way he drawled the words accused her of having lain in wait just so she could run into him accidentally on purpose. Perhaps some nurses did hurl themselves almost into the arms of a very attractive surgeon. *She* wouldn't dream of doing so. 'I mean that I didn't know you were still in Theatres,' she said proudly, chin lifting.

'Officially I'm not. But I've been watching the professor perform another miracle.'

'The by-pass heart valve insertion!' Kelly forgot to be stiff at the mention of a common interest. 'I should love to have scrubbed for that one,' she said almost wistfully. 'Cardiac surgery really fascinates me. But I didn't get the chance even to watch any of it.'

Griff liked her enthusiasm and the sudden warm spontaneity that replaced the defensive and rather defiant attitude. 'What have you been doing?' He ought to walk on, he knew. There was no point in keeping her in idle conversation, inviting Angie's wrath to fall on the new theatre nurse who she didn't seem to like very much. He wasn't really so interested in Kelly Lorimer and he felt it would be a mistake to encourage her obvious interest in himself. But he was held by the dawning smile in the beautiful hazel eyes.

She wrinkled her nose prettily. 'Tonsils and gall bladders!'

He smiled at the wry tone. 'Fleming?'

'Yes, mostly.'

'Tedious,' he sympathised, knowing the man's pain-staking slowness and his irritating habit of explaining every move he made to an experienced team. 'I expect you felt like taking over at times.'

Kelly warmed to the gleam of understanding in the grey eyes and the charm of a totally unexpected smile. 'I ought not to criticise,' she said thoughtfully. 'He's much more reliable than some of the whizz-kids who set out to break records and show off their skill and want to sew up almost before the last swab has been counted. Mr

Fleming may be slow but he's thorough, and that's what really matters.'

'I'm afraid you and I share a complaint that doesn't endear us to some members of our profession,' Griff said dryly.

'Do we?' Kelly looked doubtful but she was transparently pleased by the thought of sharing anything with a man who seemed unexpectedly disposed to be friendly.

'It's known as the Hartlake Headswell and attacks all those who train at a certain hospital in London,' he explained with the ghost of a twinkle. 'There's no cure for it, I'm afraid. I can only advise that you refrain from snatching the scalpel from the surgeon's hand no matter how tempted you are, or how strong your conviction that you can do very much better.'

She laughed up at him, eyes dancing with an absurd delight in that common bond of a Hartlake background, heart lifting at the reminder that he had a good sense of humour as well as all his other attractions.

'I suppose we are inclined to believe that we're the best in the world!'

'And so we are.' His smile embraced her with a sudden warmth and there was a kind of intimacy in the way that they looked into each other's eyes.

Angie's voice broke purposefully across a moment when they came near to a new understanding. 'I'm sure there must be something that you ought to be doing, Nurse Lorimer,' she declared in her lilting voice. 'How can you find time to gossip when everyone else is rushed off their feet, I wonder?' The words were light but barbed.

'My fault, Angie,' Griff said easily, turning with a smile for the theatre sister.

Somehow, those brown eyes managed to smile back at

the surgeon while sparking with dislike and annoyance at Kelly.

'My nurses don't need any encouragement to neglect their work,' she returned brightly. *Or to flirt with any available man*, her tone implied.

'I've finished my work for the day, Sister. I'm just going off duty,' Kelly said coolly. *And you know it perfectly well*, the hazel eyes signalled with their militant sparkle.

'Then you shouldn't be here. I've heard that Hartlake nurses are dedicated, but this is carrying your love of Theatres too far,' Angie teased with the smile that didn't reach her eyes. 'Off you go, Nurse—and don't let me see you again until tomorrow morning!'

It sounded like light-hearted dismissal by a friendly and good-natured and concerned theatre sister, but Kelly was well aware of the enmity that underlay the words, even if Griff Rydell was deceived.

He hadn't done her any favours by coming to her defence in that manner and Angie would probably complain that he was taking too much notice of a new theatre nurse, she thought wryly, standing beneath the shower while the hot water cascaded down her slender back and over her tingling breasts in a refreshing stream. Little did Angie know that the surgeon had no reason and no real wish to be nice to a newcomer who reminded him too vividly of the painful past.

She mustn't make the mistake of attaching too much importance to those few moments of friendliness, Kelly told herself sensibly. Briefly, she and Griff Rydell had been linked by a mutual interest in surgery, by the fact that she was a Hartlake nurse and he was a Hartlake man—and, whether or not he chose to remember, by the warmth of liking that they'd once known for each other.

They hadn't met so very often or for so very long in the

days when he'd been engaged to Kate, but he'd always been charming to a seventeen-year-old schoolgirl, making her feel like a woman without ever embarrassing her or exposing her tender, mixed-up, newly aroused feelings by betraying that he was aware of them. He'd been kind, good-natured and generous with his interest and his encouragement for her ambition to be a nurse, telling her about his work and initiating her love of surgery with his own enthusiasm. He'd influenced her life far more than he'd ever known, in fact, and perhaps she'd always hoped to meet him again—or someone very like him.

His niceness combined with his striking good looks, his success as a surgeon and his prowess as an athlete had made it too easy for Kelly to fancy herself in love with the attractive young surgeon. She'd been much too young and too inexperienced to suppose that she could lure him away from her lovely and sophisticated cousin. Now, he was a free agent and she was no longer so young or so innocent and she wanted him—but she still didn't know how to go about getting him, she thought ruefully.

There seemed to be too many obstacles to any real understanding between them. Her uncertain relationship with Jeremy, for one. Griff's possible involvement with Angie Howell, for another. The gulf of six years between the past and the present. His very understandable bitterness about something he wished to forget and which her arrival in Porthbryn had revived. Kelly wondered wistfully if he would like her any better if he could only forget that she was a Lorimer—and if they could ever escape from the shadow of Kate . . .

Kelly was laying up a trolley for a routine appendicectomy the next morning, while Megan and Sharon prepared the theatre, when Angie Howell hurried into the ante-room, looking visibly annoyed.

'Heaven preserve me from the whims and fancies of surgeons,' she said irritably. 'I'm afraid we have a change of schedule at short notice, Nurse Lorimer. I'm transferring your appendicectomy case to another theatre. Mr Rydell wishes to use this one for his list. I'm sure I don't know why, when one operating-room is much like any other, but I suppose we have to humour him!' The glitter in the dark eyes implied that she knew and did not approve of the surgeon's reasons for insisting on the change.

'Very well, Sister.' Kelly was careful not to sound too pleased at the thought of working with Griff on much more interesting cases than her original list for that day.

Perhaps she was slightly too demure. For Angie looked at her swiftly, with narrowed and suspicious eyes.

'Did you already know about this?' she demanded coldly. 'Were you discussing it with Griff Rydell when I caught you with him in the corridor yesterday afternoon?'

She managed to make a chance encounter sound not only clandestine but illicit, Kelly thought, bridling with indignation. 'No, Sister! It's a complete surprise to me,' she said firmly.

Angie frowned. 'I don't know that I believe you,' she said bluntly, bringing previously veiled antagonism out into the open. 'I know you're bored by routine operations and no doubt you feel that your superior talents are being wasted on them, but you ought not to persuade senior surgeons to arrange matters so that you can scrub for them, you know. I don't know how they do things at Hartlake, of course. Or Marks Cross. But it isn't *my* idea of theatre etiquette.'

With an effort, Kelly kept her temper, knowing that if she wanted to work with Griff that day or any other then she must swallow the offensive words and tone. For the theatre sister might talk of humouring surgeons but she still had ultimate authority and full responsibility for Theatres, and she could refuse to chop and change the schedules to suit one surgeon's preference for a particular operating-room and a particular scrub nurse if she chose.

'I'm afraid you overestimate my powers of persuasion where Mr Rydell is concerned,' she said coolly. 'I had nothing to do with his decision. I don't even know which cases he has on his list for this morning.'

'I must give you the benefit of the doubt, I suppose.' It was grudging, ungracious.

Kelly shrugged with the pretence of cool indifference. 'Just as you like, Sister. I'm happy to work in any theatre with any surgeon, so if you really suspect a conspiracy between myself and Mr Rydell then I think you should arrange for another nurse to scrub for him. I don't suppose he'll mind any more than I will.'

Griff strolled into the ante-room in time to hear most of the words. 'What's wrong, Angie? What's the problem?' he drawled. 'Isn't it convenient for me to use this theatre?' He nodded a careless good morning to Kelly.

'Well, it's rather naughty of you to leave it to the last moment to make changes.' Angie said with a smile for the surgeon that took the sting from the scold. 'It's really booked for Jeremy Hunt's list, you know.'

'I gather that he doesn't object to using another theatre and that his first patient hasn't yet come up from the ward.' He sounded slightly impatient. 'But if it's a nuisance then I'll work in Number One, as usual. Just let me have Nurse Lorimer. I need her experience.' He turned to Kelly. 'My first case is a partial thyroidectomy that may present some problems. I believe that you assisted Hunt with similar surgery on several occasions when you were both working at Marks Cross?'

'Yes, that's right. I'm familiar with the procedure and with the kind of complications that can arise,' Kelly agreed quietly.

Griff turned back to the smouldering Angie. 'So it has to be either Nurse Lorimer or yourself—and I understand that you're working with Harvey this morning?'

Kelly could almost sympathise with the theatre sister's dilemma. Angie was so jealous that she'd love to deny her the opportunity of working with Griff, but at the same time she was reluctant to relinquish her place on the consultant gynaecological surgeon's team. Everyone knew that she enjoyed gynae work and felt flattered by Sir Lennard's insistence that she scrub for him on his operating days at the Porthbryn General.

It wasn't unusual for a surgeon to request that a particular nurse should assist him in the theatre and so Angie's irritation was out of all proportion. Kelly wished she knew if the woman regarded her as a professional rival or as a rival for Griff's interest and affection. Then she might be able to feel that her own penchant for a very attractive surgeon wasn't entirely hopeless . . .

CHAPTER SIX

'I'VE JUST instructed Nurse Lorimer to get the theatre ready for your list.' Angie almost snapped the words. 'As you say, I am assisting Sir Lennard, and as he's due at any moment, I'll leave you in obviously capable hands.' She whisked out of the room in high dudgeon.

Kelly looked at the surgeon with a rueful smile in her hazel eyes. 'I appreciate the thought, but you weren't very tactful in your methods,' she said lightly, supposing that he'd rescued her from a morning of routine surgery because of their brief exchange on the subject the previous day.

He frowned. 'Tact doesn't come into it. I shall be performing a difficult piece of surgery and I need a theatre nurse with your experience and ability. I wasn't influenced by personal considerations of any kind.'

Colour rose in her face at the snubbing words. 'Well, *I* know that,' she rallied tartly, feeling that he'd deliberately slapped her down yet again and wishing that she hadn't spoken so impulsively. 'But Angie doesn't. She's convinced that we had it all arranged between us in advance!'

Griff shrugged broad shoulders in the thin green tunic. 'And that bothers you?'

'Not in the slightest.'

'Perhaps you are more concerned with Hunt's views in the matter? You were supposed to be working together this morning, apparently. He didn't raise any objection to losing your services as scrub nurse.'

She wanted to protest at the sardonic note in his deep

voice. She stifled the impulse and said firmly, 'I'm sure that Jeremy understands your reasons. Angie won't. I'm not one of her favourite people and she'll like me even less if you start favouring me, for whatever reason.'

'I don't make a practice of favouring any nurse above another unless it's for the benefit of a patient. I want you because I can trust your training and your practical experience.' He glanced at his watch. 'I'm told that my patient has had her pre-med and will be coming up from the ward very shortly. Can you have the theatre ready in twenty minutes?'

'Certainly, Mr Rydell.'

'Good.' He moved towards the door. 'I want to visit a patient on another ward but I'll be back in good time to scrub up and I shall expect to find everything ready for me.'

His tone was so peremptory that Kelly looked after him in surprise. He was so unpredictable and so changeable in his attitude to her, she thought wryly. Just when she thought they were on the verge of friendship he added another brick to the wall of reserve and resentment. Just like Angie, he was determined not to like her although he apparently felt compelled to make use of her theatre skills because he was a caring and conscientious surgeon who wanted only the best for his patients.

Kelly didn't care for the implication that she was a better nurse than her colleagues in Theatres but she *was* trained at Hartlake, and that seemed to count for a great deal in the profession. It was certainly obvious that Griff was prepared to put up with her as his right-hand in the theatre because of her qualifications, no matter what he thought and felt about her as a person in her own right.

An ache that was becoming much too familiar began to steal about her heart. Why on earth did it matter so much *what* he thought and felt about her? Was he becoming so important so soon, or was her hurt just a hangover from the days when she'd felt that he liked her? Or was it only a matter of pride with her to break through the barrier of undeserved resentment and force him to accept her, even if she was a Lorimer?

It was certainly a matter of pride to have the theatre ready for him when he returned to scrub up and don mask and gown and gloves, she told herself firmly, hurrying to inform Megan and Sharon and the rest of the theatre team of the unexpected change in the list.

The patient arrived with the attendant nurse and was handed over to the waiting anaesthetist and his prepared hypodermic before being trundled into the operating-room and transferred to the table, deeply unconscious and carefully monitored.

Kelly was making the last-minute check of instruments and swabs with Sharon's assistance when Griff came in, gowned and masked, and approached the group who stood about the operating-table, waiting for him.

For a moment or two he was silent, surveying the scene. He looked at the patient, already positioned on the table in readiness for surgery, and at the anaesthetist who was in the process of adjusting valves and checking dials on his complicated mass of equipment. He looked at the hovering team of nurses and technicians who knew exactly what to do and would proceed to do it at a nod from the scrub nurse, who was responsible for the running of the theatre, its cleanliness and the condition of its equipment, and the efficiency of its staff.

He looked at the trolley with its neat array of instruments—its scalpels, haemostats, retractors, clips and scissors, forceps, needle-holders and sutures and prepared hypodermic syringes. Finally, he looked directly at Kelly as she turned towards him with an enquiring and slightly anxious expression in the hazel eyes above the green mask.

Griff gave a little nod of approval and thought she relaxed. He caught the gleam of a smile in those expressive eyes before she turned back to her task.

'How's my patient, Tim?' He spoke to the busy anaesthetist.

He didn't look up. 'Well under. No respiratory or cardiovascular problems so far. She's yours if you want to begin.'

'Good. All set, Nurse Lorimer?'

'. . . thirteen, fourteen, fifteen. That should be enough. Thank you, Sharon.' Kelly finished the swab count and made a final check of the trolley. Then she said quietly, and with an echo of his impersonality, 'Yes, everything's in order. We're quite ready, Mr Rydell.'

As she spoke, Kelly wondered if the theatre team noticed how formal she and Griff were with each other and what they thought about it. First names were commonplace in Theatres where a friendly and informal atmosphere was essential to counterbalance the tension and concentration of surgery when life and health and mobility were at stake. Caught off guard, Kelly had often used his first name and was usually snubbed for doing so, she thought wryly.

'My technique differs from the orthodox, Nurse Lorimer. Perhaps I ought to run through it before we start and then you should be able to follow what I'm doing without too much difficulty.'

Kelly listened carefully as he outlined the procedure and repeated some of it to show that she had understood. Then she nodded. 'That seems quite clear, Mr Rydell.'

She saw that he was pleased with her quick grasp and she surprised a smile of approval in the grey eyes that compensated her for the earlier and perhaps unintentional hurt of his brusque words and manner. Like many surgeons, he was single-minded about his work—and she was ready to make allowances for him, if only for the sake of past acquaintance. Then, as he held out his hand for the scalpel and she watched him make the first neat incision with a swift, sure stroke, she told herself firmly to keep her mind on her own work and do her best to justify his belief in the ability and expertise of a Hartlake nurse.

When the last suture had been inserted and the patient wheeled away to the recovery room—with particular care taken to support her head in just the right position so that the sutures in the platysma muscle should remain intact—Griff stepped back from the table, peeled off his mask and ran a hand over aching eyes, looking about him with the air of a man coming up for air.

He was the kind of dedicated surgeon who became mentally and emotionally involved as well as physically engaged in the business of healing with the knife. For him, time stood still; he was only aware of himself, the patient, the automatic efficiency of the instrument nurse and the need to exercise his surgical skills to the best of his ability. It was only when the task was complete and he handed his patient into the care of the nursing staff on the ward that he realised his tension and his tiredness.

Kelly was already organising the cleaning of the theatre, the removal for sterilisation of the used instruments and bowls, the whisking away of dirty towels and drapes. The anaesthetist was closing off valves and satisfying himself that his equipment was in perfect order for the next time it would be needed.

Suddenly he was in the way, Griff thought dryly, and moved towards the ante-room, pulling off gown and mask and dropping them into the 'dirty' bin on his way.

He nodded agreement as the anaesthetist remarked that the operation had gone well, but he didn't pause to reply.

In the ante-room, he dragged the theatre cap from his head and bent over a basin to sluice cold water over his face, refreshing his skin and eyes and jaded senses. As he straightened, someone put a towel into his hands.

Pausing, Griff looked at the slender girl in the thin theatre dress. A few strands of silky fair hair escaped from beneath the mob cap and a slight smile in the lovely eyes arrested his attention. She persisted in behaving as if they were friends, he thought wearily. She reminded him of a puppy who didn't understand a well-aimed kick, even when it was flying through the air. But Kelly was stubborn rather than unsuspecting in her refusal to accept that she was an unwelcome intruder into the life that he'd rearranged to his satisfaction.

'Thanks . . .' He held the towel to his face.

Elated and slightly euphoric after working with a brilliant surgeon and feeling that she'd acquitted herself well, Kelly had followed him from the operating-room on a sudden impulse to voice her admiration for his surgical skill. She was briefly disconcerted by the lack of warmth in the way he looked and spoke. Then she reminded herself that he'd been working at full stretch and was obviously tired.

She said warmly, 'That was very well done, you know. It might not have been textbook surgery but it was certainly very clever.'

'Put it in writing and I'll have it framed,' he drawled dryly.

Kelly flushed at the sardonic tone. 'Did it sound like a well-meaning pat on the head? I'm sorry. I didn't mean to patronise you,' she said stiffly, making matters worse.

He looked at her with the glint of mockery in his grey

eyes. 'How could you? Even you couldn't have done it better.'

Kelly managed to laugh as if she believed it to be gentle teasing when it was only too obvious that he was keeping her at a distance with that snubbing sarcasm.

'Don't be horrid, Griff! You know what I'm trying to say and you're making me say it very badly,' she reproached brightly.

'So you're impressed.' He shrugged. 'Every surgeon has his party piece. That just happens to be mine,' he said carelessly.

He rubbed at his wet hair with the towel as he spoke and Kelly thought how much younger and more approachable he suddenly seemed with that tangle of dark curls falling across his handsome brow. She felt an inexplicable and increasingly familiar tug at her heart, as well as the unmistakable stirring of physical attraction, and hastily dropped her gaze as he caught her watching him with far too much interest and admiration.

'Well, I'm glad you allowed me to help you with your party piece on this occasion,' she said as lightly as she could for her discomfiture.

Griff raised an eyebrow. 'You're too modest, Nurse Lorimer. I don't know how I'd have managed without you.'

She smiled wryly. 'Don't let Angie hear you say so. She might think that you mean it!'

'Do you think you can do as well with this afternoon's sigmoidostomy? You'll have a couple of hours to read up on it if you aren't too sure, but it's a fairly straight-forward op once we get into the colon.'

Kelly hesitated. 'Sister Howell will be free to scrub for you this afternoon. Apparently, Sir Lennard will have his list finished before lunch.'

He frowned. 'Are you off duty?'

'No, but . . .'

'Then you'll be in charge of this theatre and it's your job to scrub for the surgeons who use it. That's right, isn't it?'

'Yes, but . . .'

'Are you afraid of a simple sigmoidostomy?'

'Of course I'm not!' she said indignantly.

'Then it's settled. The patient comes up at two-thirty.'

Kelly had made a token protest but she was pleased that he'd brushed it aside so peremptorily. But it would be nice to be wanted for something more than her theatre experience, she thought wistfully, and then hastily dragged her thoughts from that dangerous path.

'I'll leave you to settle it with Sister,' she said dryly.

'No problem,' Griff said confidently. He tossed the used towel into the bin and strolled to the door. 'Make sure that you have a good lunch and relax for an hour before coming back to theatre,' he advised. 'It'll be a busy afternoon for both of us.'

He'd sounded really concerned, Kelly thought, surprised. The man was an enigma, totally unpredictable. But at least he admired her work and that might pave the way to friendship between them in time, she thought with her usual optimism.

She didn't want to think that he might never warm to her or wish to know her beyond the aseptic and rather unromantic setting of Theatres. Or that while she might occasionally oust Angie from her place at the surgeon's side in an operating-room, she might never oust her from a place she seemed to enjoy in his affections and his life . . .

Kelly took his advice and read up on procedure and technique before she met Jeremy for lunch in the staff cafeteria. The operation was one that she hadn't seen since her training days and she was determined not to make any mistakes.

Jeremy was interested in hearing all about the morning and not at all surprised that his colleague had wanted her assistance. He was pleased that she was bearing out all his previous praise of her ability and efficiency. She enjoyed an hour with him, when she felt like a woman as well as a theatre nurse, and returned for the afternoon's work bolstered by the warmth of his affection and concern and good wishes.

The sigmoidostomy was as straightforward and as successful as Griff had promised. He took it for granted that she knew which instrument he would require before he held out his hand for it or spoke, that she didn't need to be told what to do and when to do it, and that she was as familiar as himself with the operation. There wasn't a word or a smile of approval as he turned from the table.

Kelly felt she'd done well but she didn't forget the importance of the back-up provided by the rest of the theatre team. She made a point of thanking them and praising their work before she turned her back on Theatres for the weekend.

Griff was standing by the lift as she emerged, her hair still damp from the shower and swinging lightly on her shoulders, a glow in her cheeks. He turned to look at her and Kelly's heart lifted with the foolish and unlikely hope that he'd been waiting for her. She smiled at him, the swift, sweet smile that was more effective than she knew, with its endearing hint of shyness.

As the lift doors slid back, he ushered her before him with an almost peremptory jerk of his dark head. Standing by his side in the unusually empty lift, Kelly was much too conscious of his physical presence and her own response to it. The crisp black curls on the nape of his

neck tempted her to touch them. She longed to trace
with tender fingers the faint but distinctive scar that
streaked his lean cheek. The need to touch him in some
way was so urgent that it was alarming. So was the
sudden yearning to have his arms about her and to know
the warmth of his kiss and the urgency of his hard body
against her own.

Her heart thumped as he turned his head to look at
her, as though he sensed the stir of her emotions. Her
instinct abruptly alerted her to danger, warning her that
a sensual surgeon was finding her just as disturbing in
that entirely physical way. The tension between them
while the lift carried them downwards was almost
unbearable—and quite unmistakable.

'Hunt and I were just talking about you,' he said
abruptly. 'Did you never think of medicine and possible
surgery rather than nursing?'

'Heavens, no! I just wanted to nurse.' Kelly was
grateful that he'd broken the silence and the growing
tension. She was surprised that he and the still-working
Jeremy had been talking her over and she was rather
flattered by the implication that she might have been
capable of doing their difficult and demanding work if
she'd had the training.

'Pity. But you haven't the build for it, of course,' Griff
commented, as impersonally as if he was unmoved by
the tiny waist and small, tilting breasts and the air of
fragile femininity that tugged so strongly at his senses as
well as arousing all his protective instincts, despite his
resolution to avoid becoming involved in any way with
the pretty Kelly Lorimer. 'You're too slight for surgery.
It takes more physical strength and stamina to operate
for several hours at a stretch than most people realise. I
expect that's one of the reasons why few women special-
ise in surgery.' He smiled slightly. 'At the risk of sound-

ing chauvinist, I must admit that I regard it as a man's job.'

'But I think *you* must find it a strain at times,' Kelly said gently, thinking of his spinal injury, the several operations and the long convalescence, sure that he wasn't always free of the reminder of pain and weakness.

Griff shrugged, impatient with the hint of a sympathy he didn't need or want from anyone. 'I'm doing the job I was trained to do instead of sitting in a wheelchair. That's all that I care about. There's a lot of satisfaction in going home exhausted at the end of a good day's work in the theatre after being told at one time that my career as a surgeon was finished.'

'When did you come to Porthbryn?' As a senior surgeon, he was respected and admired but he didn't seem to be very well known. Or perhaps no one talked much about him because he'd been around too long to be interesting?

'Soon after it opened. It was my first surgical appointment for some time and I felt a temporary job in a new and not too busy hospital would prove whether or not I was fit to stand the pace. I liked the place and the people and found I could handle the work even when we became busy, so I decided to stay and make my home here.'

She nodded. 'It's a long way from London,' she said tentatively, thinking of his family and his friends and the lifestyle he'd once known and enjoyed. 'Don't you miss it, Griff?'

'I don't miss it at all. Or its associations ' He spoke with a snap of finality that warned her to abandon the subject.

Kelly stepped out of the lift and began to cross Main Hall towards the wide expanse of glass doors, wanting to get out into the sunshine and fresh air as soon as possible after long hours in theatre, although it was a roundabout route to the car park. She was surprised when the surgeon fell into step at her side. She wondered if he really wanted to walk with her or if he was merely being polite.

He had certainly been more communicative than usual and Kelly was encouraged by that slight lowering of reserve. Maybe he was beginning to accept that it wasn't her fault that she was a Lorimer and to feel that they should be on friendly terms as they would obviously be working together so much, she thought hopefully.

'You're not resident, are you?' She tried to make it sound casual rather than curious, although she was longing to know where he lived—and if he lived alone. For all she knew, he shared a home and a very intimate relationship with the proprietorial Angie Howell! But it would surely be common knowledge if it was so, she decided with a strange kind of comfort in the thought.

'Not now. I've just bought a cottage in Penbryn.'

Griff named a village on the coast just a short distance from the farm, and she looked up quickly and with interest. He had to pass the caravan on his way to and from the hospital, she realised, and that made them almost neighbours!

She passed through the swing door as he held it open and then paused on the top step, appreciating the freshness of the air, impulsively lifting her face to the sun. Griff looked at her with a sudden smile for that youthful reaction to a day that held the promise of glorious summer. She sent him a swift, slightly shy smile from dancing hazel eyes—a smile that held so much unconscious enchantment that he was abruptly jolted into renewed awareness of her as an attractive and exciting and wholly desirable woman.

It was some time since he'd known such a fierce

kindling of his emotions. The glow in the expressive eyes and the almost tangible tension in her slight frame as their eyes met and held, told him that he had only to say the right word, make the right move, and they would take the first step towards a relationship—with all its inevitable consequences.

Tempted, Griff hesitated. She was hurling herself at him on a whirlwind of sentiment that had its roots in the past rather than the present, he felt. She was remembering the man he had been, knowing little of the man he'd become, and she was too impulsive, too intense and much too vulnerable. It would be so easy to reach out and take all she offered with that smile, the look in her lovely eyes, but he was afraid that he'd hurt her in the process. She was the type who fell in love, he thought ruefully, and that was the last thing he wanted.

But he wanted *her*. God, how he wanted her! The desire surged like molten flame through his veins for this slender girl with her pale hair and pretty face and shining eyes. He dug his hands deep into his pockets to prevent himself from reaching out to her, making a move that he knew they would both regret.

For he had nothing to give any woman these days but the doubtful satisfaction of a brief and entirely sexual encounter and he knew instinctively that a girl like Kelly Lorimer would demand much more than that of him . . .

CHAPTER SEVEN

MEETING THE surgeon's eyes for a timeless and supercharged moment, Kelly's heart lurched. A tingling tremor quivered all the way down her spine in a sudden electrifying shock of excitement and longing . . . and something more.

It was only a few days since she'd met him again, but he threatened to have a lasting effect on her emotions, she admitted with a thump of a heart that wasn't sure it wanted to give itself so soon and so irrevocably to a man who didn't seem to want it.

But she wanted and needed his friendship and so she clutched at the straw of unexpected warmth in his smile and said with dangerous impulsiveness, 'I live on the Penbryn road, Griff. I've rented a caravan at Caradoc Farm. You must have seen it from the road . . . a little box on wheels! If you're on your way home, why don't you come and have some tea with me? I'll introduce you to the cows who share the field!'

It was light—warm friendliness rather than blatant invitation—but a guarded expression touched the grey eyes and Kelly knew that she'd taken too much for granted because of something she might only have imagined in the way that he'd held her gaze with his own and smiled.

Now, the smile had fled and she saw the muscles in his lean jaw suddenly tighten. 'Perhaps I'm old-fashioned, but I feel that a man should still be allowed to make the running, even in these topsy-turvy days when women have things all their own way and want to rule the world,' he drawled with a mocking edge to the words. 'Wait for me to do the asking and then you can have the privilege of saying yes or no. It's the way it should be, in my chauvinistic view.'

Following immediately on a smile that had almost whisked her heart from her breast, his words and manner were a slap in the face for poor Kelly. She stared at him, face flaming, temporarily silenced by shock and humiliation and leaping anger. Before she could rally and frame a crushing retort, he hailed a passing acquaintance and moved away from her. Kelly didn't feel the usual tug of compassion as she observed the slight drag of that long left leg.

She was much too angry.

She walked rapidly towards the car park with a chill about her heart that no amount of sun could possibly thaw, still trembling from the shock of those brutally blunt words from a man she'd been too ready to like. She was desperately hurt because he'd so obviously wanted to punish her for what another woman had done to him six years before. She was a Lorimer and she reminded him too painfully of the past and that was apparently enough cause to snub and insult her as often as he chose, she thought bitterly.

She *wasn't* running after him, as he had unmistakably and offensively implied with those mocking words. She liked him and she was sorry that he'd been hurt in heart and mind and body—but that was all!

For the second time he'd made her feel cheap and pushy and she burned with humiliation and indignation. Was he so spoiled by a succession of women who'd found him physically attractive and shown it too plainly, that he couldn't recognise ordinary liking and friendly interest when it was offered? Well, she wouldn't try again to bridge the gulf that he deliberately widened at every opportunity. He was a hard and vindictive man with a crushing arrogance and a vitriolic tongue and she determined that he wouldn't get another chance to slap her down.

Those harsh, horrid words would ring in her ears and sting her feelings for a long time, but she hoped that she had too much pride to let him or any other man know that he had the power to hurt her so badly.

Thank heavens for Jeremy! Griff Rydell couldn't run away with the idea that she fancied him once he realised the extent of her involvement with another man—and it would be the easiest thing in the world to make him aware of it. She hadn't meant to rush into the total commitment that Jeremy wanted from her, but it would serve as a smokescreen and surely it must stamp out the stupid weakness that was threatening to destroy her happiness and peace of mind.

Kelly was reluctant to admit it, but she'd come dangerously close to falling in love with Griff Rydell. She'd been a little in love with the memory of the man for six years, of course. Meeting him again had seemed so right and so romantic that her impulsive heart had almost launched itself at a man who didn't like her or want her at all—and didn't hesitate to tell her so!

She might have rushed headlong into Jeremy's arms that very night. But they hadn't arranged to meet and she was reluctant to turn up at his flat without invitation or warning, friends though they were.

For one thing, Angie might be there. Kelly couldn't rid herself of the conviction that the attractive brunette was playing one man off against the other and she still wasn't sure which of them Angie really wanted—or how either of them felt about Angie.

For another . . . well, she mustn't make the mistake of throwing herself at a man's head twice in one day, she thought bitterly, knowing that Jeremy would certainly be suspicious of her motives if she invited his lovemaking after so many refusals.

'Kelly!'

She spun at the sound of her name, too eagerly, too ready to forgive and forget. Her foolish heart plunged with disappointment as she saw John Duncan hurrying to catch up with her. But she found a smile for him, hoping that it was convincing camouflage for the way she was feeling. She liked the young anaesthetist who'd felt like a friend from their first meeting. It was obvious that he liked her, too. He'd taken several opportunities in the last few days to let her know that she was in his thoughts, even if they were both too busy in different theatres to do more than smile or exchange a friendly word in passing.

He certainly wasn't the kind to say cold, cutting things to a girl just to hurt and humiliate her and keep her at arm's length, she thought, still smarting. He was a dear and if she ever wanted or needed a replacement for Jeremy, she might do much worse than turn to someone who made no secret of his admiration and interest.

'I'm glad I caught you,' he said warmly. 'I saw you with Griff Rydell and then you dashed away as if all the hounds of hell were after you!'

'I'm in a bit of a rush . . .'

'I won't keep you more than a moment. I hoped to have a word with you in Theatres but you'd gone by the time I was free to look for you.'

'What can I do for you?' She sent him an encouraging smile.

'You're in a hurry. Do you have a date?'

Kelly hesitated. 'Not exactly . . .'

'Could you come to a party? Would you like to, Kelly?'

'A party?'

'Oh, nothing grand. Just a few people at a friend's place—a birthday party for his girlfriend. A drink or two, some music and a lot of "shop", I expect. I think you'll enjoy it.' His smile was warm and coaxing. 'Do come.'

The invitation was unexpected and it came at just the right moment to apply a little balm to her wounded feelings. Kelly might have turned down a dinner invitation but a party was a different matter. It was certainly preferable to spending the evening alone in the caravan with thoughts of Griff Rydell's behaviour to disturb and depress her, she decided.

'I'd love to come,' she said promptly.

'You won't be among strangers,' he promised. 'Gary is a houseman on Houghton Ward and Penny works as a physiotherapist here at the hospital. There's sure to be one or two people who you know—and you'll know everyone else by the time the party breaks up.'

Kelly looked beyond the anaesthetist at the tall figure who was just entering the car park. He glanced with apparent indifference in their direction. Instantly, she moved closer to John and put a hand on his arm and smiled up into his eyes with much more warmth than she'd intended. 'It sounds lovely. Where shall we meet, and what time?'

Having agreed that he should call for her at the caravan and given him the address, Kelly got into her Mini and drove out of the car park just ahead of Griff's dark blue saloon. In fact, she shot in front of him deliberately, forcing him to slam on the brakes, and saw his handsome face darken with annoyance as she glanced in the rear mirror.

Halting briefly before driving out into the stream of traffic on the coast road, Kelly was punished for that petty satisfaction when the Mini suddenly stalled. Griff's was not the only car behind her and as she'd been preparing to turn right she was blocking the gateway so that no car could overtake. She tried unsuccessfully to get the engine to turn over again while one impatient motorist tooted his horn and passers-by looked at her in sympathy or amusement. She was tired and strung-up and exasperated with the car that had been so temperamental since she brought it to North Wales, and she almost snapped at the well-meaning porter who strolled from the lodge to say kindly, 'Sounds like she's flooded, Nurse.'

'I'm tempted to push her over the cliff and let her drown,' she said bitterly, thrusting the mass of pale hair from her face with a weary hand.

He grinned. 'Let's just push her to the side for now and let these other drivers get by, shall we?'

Kelly sighed. 'Yes, I suppose so.'

'Give her a few minutes to dry out,' he advised. 'They're good little cars when they're looked after but you can't afford to neglect them. Just like women, I always say . . .'

'Do you propose to park here all night, Nurse Lorimer?' Griff's tone was brusque and irritated as he came up to the car to investigate the hold-up.

'The nurse's car has stalled, sir.'

Kelly didn't look at the surgeon. 'I'd move it if I could,' she said angrily.

'We're just proposing to push it out of the way, sir,' the porter assured him, pouring oil.

'I advise you to do nothing of the kind,' Griff said grimly. 'It isn't three months since I had you in the theatre for a hernia and I've no desire to see you there again.' He bent down to Kelly. 'For God's sake, get out of that heap and let me see what I can do!'

'You can go to hell,' she said, low and furious.

'Not in that car, thanks. I'd be lucky if it took me as far as the town centre. Come on—get out!'

For answer, she sent up a silent prayer and tried the key in a last, desperate attempt. To her relief, the engine caught and quickened.

'That's it, miss! You'll be all right now! Just keep it going,' Joe said quickly and stepped hastily out of the way as the car jerked a few feet.

Griff turned away with a shrug of broad shoulders as she thankfully edged the car forward. She still couldn't escape for a steady stream of traffic was blocking her right turn and she had to wait for a gap between cars. But at least there was now sufficient clearance for a car to pass on her left. In her rear mirror, she watched Griff slide behind the wheel of his saloon and set it in motion, and then he drove past without a glance for her or the Mini.

She'd expected him to turn right too, heading for Penbryn, but perhaps he wasn't going home. Perhaps he was hurrying to join Angie, who'd gone off duty early that afternoon.

She drove along the coast road, mentally reviewing her wardrobe for something suitable for a party and refusing to think about the surgeon. Then, halted by traffic lights at a junction, she saw the dark-blue car waiting to turn right and realised that he'd taken a detour. Slightly and foolishly flustered, she began to move off on the amber, realised she was jumping the lights and hastily slammed on the brakes. As the light changed to green, she trod on the accelerator but the Mini took exception to the stop-go treatment and promptly sat down on her haunches and refused to budge. Kelly could have cried with temper and frustration as she struggled to start the engine all over again while the lights changed back to red. She didn't know or care if Griff was aware of her plight and she certainly didn't expect him to come to her aid. So she was surprised when he suddenly appeared at the open car window and drawled, 'This is getting to be a habit. I told you this wreck needed major surgery.'

He'd found it impossible to drive on and abandon her. She was such a pretty damsel in such obvious distress and he'd had time to regret the rebuff that he'd handed out in sheer self-defence. Knowing that he'd been too hard on her and feeling that he could have handled the situation so much better, he was almost glad of an opportunity to redeem himself to some extent.

Kelly glowered, resenting the gleam of sardonic amusement in the grey eyes and failing to recognise the offered olive branch. 'I don't need your advice or your assistance,' she said stonily. 'Just go away, will you! I can do without you on a good day!'

At that point, two men from the car behind came up, eager to help. There was a sudden flurry of male activity and discussion while Kelly sat in the car, looking and feeling helpless. Then a tow-rope was produced and attached and she found herself eased out of the driving seat while the Mini was towed by Griff's sleekly purring Jaguar into a lay-by, out of harm's way.

The obliging motorist and his friend drove on with a toot of the horn and a friendly wave. Kelly looked after them, furious that she'd been forced to accept Griff Rydell's help by well-meaning strangers and refusing to feel grateful.

Griff investigated the state of the engine but it was soon obvious that its condition was beyond his fairly comprehensive knowledge of car mechanics. He glanced at the girl who watched him in silence, noting the militant sparkle in her hazel eyes and the stubborn set to her mouth. He felt a flicker of impatience with her attitude. He was tired and pain shafted from the damaged sciatic nerve that still gave trouble at the end of a day in theatre. She was sulking, he decided. Just like a woman! Well, he was doing his best to atone, but he was damned if he'd grovel for any woman's forgiveness. Even one as pretty as Kelly Lorimer . . .

He shut down the bonnet. 'There's nothing I can do,' he said firmly. 'It's on its last legs. It needs to be taken to a garage for repair. There's one in Penbryn but you won't get a mechanic to come out tonight, I'm afraid. It should be safe enough here for the night. Lock up and I'll take you home.'

Kelly stiffened at the peremptory tone. She drew herself up to her full five foot two and looked at him coldly. 'You've been very good,' she said haughtily. 'But you mustn't give me any more of your time. I'll get a bus.'

He shrugged. 'Just as you wish. But they aren't too frequent and I'm driving past the door.'

For the sake of convenience and for no other reason, Kelly swallowed her pride. 'Very well. Thank you.' She stalked past him to the parked Jaguar and then had to wait, fuming, while he approached leisurely, got into the car and leaned across to unlock the passenger door.

She sat straight and stiff and silent while he drove, gazing at the cliffs and the glimpses of foam-crested sea as the road dipped and climbed along the coast.

But out of the corner of her eye, she saw and admired the strong, handsome profile and the confident hands on the wheel. And, despite her annoyance and her resolve not to be influenced by his looks or his charisma, she was very conscious of the man at her side and wished she could regard him as a friend instead of a disturbing threat to her peace of mind.

Griff halted the car outside the farmhouse and his eyes narrowed as he saw the tiny, white-painted caravan that was just visible through the five-barred gate of the adjoining field.

'Is that where you're living?' he demanded in blatant disapproval.

Her chin tilted at his tone. 'That's right. Home sweet home,' she said blithely.

'Alone?'

'I have the cows for company and I prefer them to some human beings,' she said pointedly.

'They won't be much protection if you get an unwelcome visitor one night.'

She frowned. 'You and Jeremy should form a company,' she said crossly. 'He's always saying the same thing. I don't know why you both feel it necessary to frighten me out of living my life the way I want!'

Griff turned in his seat to regard her thoughtfully. 'Hunt disapproves, does he? I'm not surprised. Is that really the way you want to live?'

'Of course it is!' Kelly was beginning to have her own doubts, but a streak of obstinacy refused to let her admit them so soon. It was only a week since she'd moved into the caravan and she was determined to give it a fair trial. Besides, she'd paid a month's rent in advance!

'It strikes me as utterly irresponsible,' he declared bluntly.

She bridled. 'It isn't any of your business!'

'You're an extremely pretty girl,' he told her, so impatiently that it wasn't a compliment. 'And much too trusting and impulsive, in my opinion. There are plenty of unscrupulous men on the look-out for girls like you, living on your own in the middle of nowhere with no one to keep an eye on you. You're asking for trouble and you'll probably get it.'

Kelly opened the car door. 'Thanks for the warning. But I do know something about men and their motives,' she said dryly. 'And I can look after myself. I may be impulsive and trusting but I'm not an absolute idiot!'

As she walked towards the caravan, the Jaguar shot away at speed, heading for Penbryn. Kelly didn't look after the car but her thoughts went with the surgeon. She hadn't thanked him for his assistance, she realised. She hadn't been grateful or gracious, in fact. But he didn't endear himself with that brusque arrogance or that typically male attitude to the idea of a girl living on her own without a man's protection and support. At the same time, it was kind of him to be concerned. Kind and unexpected.

Sometimes, she felt that he was drawn towards liking her but determined to resist it because of her relationship to Kate and his memories of the past. She might understand but it didn't make it hurt any less that he continued to keep her at that cool distance.

Anxious about the Mini, so useful if not very reliable of late, and ruffled by her clashes with Griff Rydell, she didn't feel much like going to the party as promised, but there was no way of letting John know that she'd changed her mind. So she was ready and waiting when he arrived for her later that evening.

They reached his friend's house on the other side of Porthbryn to find the party in full swing. Kelly was pleased to see a few familiar faces among the crowd. It was a bigger affair than John had led her to believe and people were sitting on the stairs and overflowing into the garden of the small terraced house. There was plenty to eat and drink, music that was rather too loud for comfortable conversation and a number of flirtations under way. It had all the hallmarks of a very successful party, in fact.

Kelly was glad that she'd decided to wear the new and fashionable striped silk camisole top and matching skirt with her high-heeled sandals. Like most nurses, she liked to wear something pretty and feminine when she shed her uniform on social occasions and she welcomed an opportunity to let her hair down . . . in more ways than one. She was a trifle vain about her long, ash-blonde hair with its deep, shining waves and its tendency to curl at the tips, and for much of the time its beauty was concealed by the regulation theatre cap.

It was such a warm evening that after an hour or so of circulating, Kelly was thankful to escape the heat and the noise of the room for a few minutes on the stone-paved patio while John went to fetch her a cool drink.

Lifting her long hair from her neck with both hands and sweeping it about her head in a youthful gesture, she looked up at the moon gliding in luminous beauty across the black velvet sky. For no real reason, she suddenly thought of Jeremy and wondered what he was doing that evening and if he would mind very much when he heard that she'd come to this party with John Duncan.

She'd half-expected him to turn up with Angie in tow and she wondered why she wasn't really jealous of the theatre sister. After all, *she'd* been the only girl in Jeremy's life until he came to Porthbryn. She *ought* to be jealous. Kelly wondered ruefully how and when and why her feelings had changed so completely. Had it really happened all in a moment when she met Griff Rydell again after six years of scarcely giving him a second thought?

At the sound of John's voice behind her, she turned with a smile for him that faded abruptly as she saw his companion. Their eyes met and held for a moment and she thought there was a glimmer of mocking amusement in those dark depths.

To shrink from another encounter with the surgeon would be a betrayal of the worst possible kind, she told herself firmly. He mustn't know that his presence at a party could affect her enjoyment of the evening one way or another. So she pinned her smile firmly back in place as the two men came out of the house to join her in the garden.

She bitterly regretted that she'd accepted an invitation without first finding out what it might entail. She'd leaped too quickly, as usual! But she could scarcely blame the well-meaning anaesthetist for bringing her to a party to which Griff Rydell had also been invited, she admitted fairly.

He wasn't to know that a state of war existed between herself and the surgeon . . .

CHAPTER EIGHT

GRIFF DIDN'T seem to know it either, she thought crossly, as he nodded a greeting as casually and as easily as if nothing had occurred to make the moment of meeting at all awkward or embarrassing.

John abruptly turned back into the house at a call from a friend and the surgeon moved on to join Kelly at the edge of the patio, a slender figure bathed in a shaft of moonlight that touched her pale hair to silver.

'All by yourself in the moonlight?' he asked, a glance of appraisal and approval sweeping over the bare shoulders and the hug of the camisole and the fashionably short skirt, the way she'd coaxed her hair to curl about her face and on her shoulders, the careful make-up that enhanced her delicately fair prettiness. 'Someone's missed an opportunity . . .'

There was the hint of a smile that could heal the breach then and there if she chose—or so it seemed to imply. He thought he could do and say the unforgivable and get away with it, Kelly thought indignantly, whipping up an anger that was inexplicably dying on her and refusing to admit to a sneaking delight at his presence at this party.

She made no reply but the tilt of her chin and the sparkle in her eyes expressed scorn. Then John emerged from the house once more, carrying her glass of lemonade, and she turned to him, stretching out her hand for it and thanking him with the warm sweetness of her smile.

'Just what I needed,' she said gratefully.

'Everything all right, Kelly? Enjoying yourself?'

'Very much.' She sparkled for him with a very different brilliance. 'It's a great party.'

The smile that flickered about Griff's sensual mouth mocked her enthusiasm. She threw him a swift glance that challenged him to comment and the smile deepened just a little.

'I'm glad you came.' John put an arm about her waist and gave her a little hug, friendly rather than proprietorial. Kelly leaned against him briefly, smiling up at him, warmly encouraging for the watching surgeon's benefit.

Griff moved to the edge of the patio and thrust his hands into the pockets of his jacket as he contemplated the moonlit gardens. He was impressive and very attractive with the eerie glow bathing his proud head and handsome features and tall figure. Kelly was impressed and attracted all over again, despite her resolution to ignore the persistent tug at her tumbled emotions. Her foolish heart wrenched with sudden longing as she looked at that broad, indifferent back.

'We're running low on some drinks so Gary and I are just dashing down to the local pub for reinforcements,' John said lightly. 'Can I leave you and Griff to look after each other for ten minutes or so?'

The surgeon turned, nodded assent.

Kelly said quickly, 'Don't worry about me. I'll be fine . . .' She spoke to John, but the proud assurance was meant for another man's ears.

'Sure you will,' John agreed. 'But I'll feel happier about leaving you if I know that Griff is taking good care of you for me.' He beamed on them both like a benevolent uncle, apparently unaware of her dismay and annoyance.

'Ready, John?' Their host appeared at the open window.

'I'm on my way!' He smiled reassuringly at Kelly. 'I won't be long. Talk to Griff,' he said, dropping his voice slightly. 'He seems a bit low this evening . . .' Then he turned away to join his waiting friend.

Dislike of being left with a man she hadn't wanted to encounter again so soon was written all over her as she looked at him with a proud lift to her chin and annoyance in her expressive eyes. But for some reason, it simply didn't occur to Kelly that she had only to follow the anaesthetist into the house and mingle with some of her fellow-guests to escape the discomfort of the situation.

Griff smiled at her suddenly with a little amusement and a lot of understanding. She was so pretty, so vulnerable and so touchingly transparent . . . and he wanted her very much. He was aching to hold her, to kiss that sweet mouth, to make ardent and exciting and wholly satisfying love to the stubborn and spirited girl who seemed to be drawing him like a magnet, despite his natural reluctance to have anything to do with another Lorimer.

Kelly looked at him uncertainly, not sure what his smile meant to convey but wishing that it didn't set her pulses racing in such foolish fashion. He was the most attractive man but he was also unpredictable, unreachable and possibly unreliable where women were concerned these days—and no doubt she was a fool to feel that he might be forgiven almost anything in return for the smile that seemed to be such a threat to her unsettled heart.

He moved towards her. 'Talk to Griff,' he drawled, slightly mocking, echoing words that he hadn't been meant to hear. 'Or you'll disappoint our well-meaning friend.'

Kelly refused to thaw, despite the smile that lingered in his eyes. 'I don't think I want to talk to you,' she said coolly.

'Then you don't want to hear that I've arranged for the repair of your car?'

She was startled, pleased but irritated by the sense of obligation that he was thrusting upon her with his intervention. 'When did you do that?'

'On my way home. Len Williams of Penbryn Motors has agreed to work over the weekend on your car as a special favour to me. I told him that you need the Mini to get to and from the hospital. He won't promise anything until he's had a look at the engine, of course. But he'll do his best to put it right as soon as possible. Perhaps you'll let him have the keys first thing in the morning?'

'Yes, of course. Thanks very much. It's very kind of you,' she said stiffly.

There was a twinkle in the eyes that compelled her to meet them with the sheer force of his personality. 'It sticks in your throat to say so, doesn't it?' he sympathised. 'You aren't liking me very much at the moment, I'm afraid. I don't blame you for that. I did trample all over your feelings this afternoon.'

'Yes, you did. And I suppose that's as near as you'll come to an apology,' she said tartly. But she was surprised and disarmed by the unexpected admission.

He shrugged. 'Actions are more convincing than mere words. I knew you were anxious about the Mini and thought I could do you a good turn by stopping at the garage and using my influence with Len.'

'Well, I'm grateful to you for that.' There was rather more warmth in her manner, for she realised that the local garage wouldn't have put any extra effort into a job for a stranger. She only hoped that she could afford the major repair to the Mini.

'Then I'm forgiven?'

'Why were you so horrid?' she demanded impulsively. 'I only invited you for tea, after all.'

'Tea and sympathy,' he amended dryly. 'You're a nice girl and I expect you mean well, but I don't need you or anyone else to feel sorry for me.'

She shook her head. 'You misunderstood my motives,' she said swiftly.

Griff looked down at her for a long moment, thoughtful. 'I wonder if *you* understood them? Was it really only tea that you were offering? I think it was something more, you know,' he said quietly.

So he *had* been aware of that tingling excitement, that sudden yearning, that longing to love and be loved that his nearness and the memory of his niceness had evoked. Kelly felt her face flame with embarrassment and humiliation.

'Don't flatter yourself!' she snapped.

For answer, Griff slid his hands through the silk fall of her long hair to cradle her head while he took possession of her soft mouth for a moment, finding the response he'd expected in the way that her lips warmed and quivered beneath his own. With a considerable effort of will, he resisted the impulse to allow himself to linger, to enfold her in his arms. It was neither the time nor the place, he thought wryly.

Kelly stepped back from him in instant and instinctive recoil. His kiss, with all its promise of delight, had set her trembling and tingling from head to toe. She ought to be angry with him, but she couldn't feel anything but the longing for him to kiss her again, to hold her close and sweep her with him to the wonderful world of enchantment that they could surely find in each other's arms.

'I call that adding insult to injury,' she said as coldly as she could. But there was a betraying little tremor to her voice.

Griff knew that she was trying very hard to be furious with him and he sympathised with the turmoil of her emotions if it was anything like his own. He suspected that she was torn between an instinctive attraction for himself and her loyalty to Jeremy Hunt. For his part, he was torn between wanting her and the conviction that it would be a mistake to become involved with Kate's pretty cousin. But she was all enchanting and irresistible temptation, he thought wryly, his body stirring with the beginning of desire. He smiled down at her with understanding.

'No woman is ever insulted because a man wants her and shows it. Only when he fails to want her. I think you know perfectly well how I feel about you.'

'Don't be absurd . . .' Kelly felt that he knew far too much about women and their emotions. She searched his handsome face for some sign that he meant all that he implied with the way he looked and spoke. Meeting the glow in his eyes, sensing the growing tension in his tall frame, her heart quickened and began to beat high and fast in her throat.

'You aren't a child, Kelly!' It was impatient. 'You know what you do to a man with those eyes and that smile and your lovely body. So don't pretend to be unaware of the feelings you arouse in me.' Reaching for her, he drew her close on a sudden surge of fierce wanting. 'I want you very much,' he said urgently, harsh with the intensity of his desire.

Kelly drew back in sudden alarm from the unmistakable throb of meaning in the words and the equally unmistakable throb of passion in the hard body against her own. Suddenly he was going too fast for her, urging her towards the kind of relationship that she'd avoided entering into with any man so far. The real danger lay in her own eager response to that tumultuous passion, she thought wryly. And there was even more danger in the apparent readiness of her heart to give itself irrevocably to loving.

'I think you must have had too much to drink, Mr Rydell,' she declared lightly, resorting to flippancy.

'God, no! I'm driving. Do you really think I'd risk doing to someone else what some drunken idiot did to me!' It was low, emphatic, decidedly bitter.

Kelly cursed her tactless tongue. Her heart moved with compassion and she impulsively laid her hand along the lean, scarred cheek and smiled her regret for the thoughtlessly-spoken words. 'I'm sorry, Griff. I didn't mean to remind you . . .'

He smiled wryly. 'You remind me every time I look at you. It's a little hard to take at times, but it doesn't stop me wanting you.' He drew her hand from his cheek and held it captive in strong fingers. 'I haven't wanted any woman this much in a very long time,' he said quietly.

The glow in his eyes and the passion that seemed to emanate from him sent a tremor of excitement tumbling through her slender frame. The ardent words quickened her heart with a wild and very foolish hope and she looked up at him with a swift, sweet smile and a hint of shyness in her lovely eyes.

Griff frowned suddenly. 'I'm not talking about love,' he said abruptly, dispelling illusions. 'Let's get that straight from the start. I won't dress up what I feel with lies and I won't make promises that I might not be able to keep.'

Kelly's heart felt bruised by the blunt words with their even blunter implication. She disengaged her hand and moved away from him to stand in the shadows so that her hurt shouldn't be seen in her too-expressive face. She folded her arms tightly across the ache in her breast and fought the prick of tears behind her eyes, almost wishing that she'd never come to Porthbryn. Meeting Griff Rydell again had opened the door to heartache and humiliation rather than the happiness she'd hoped, she thought bleakly.

'Are you cold?' he asked quickly, with concern, observing the way she hugged herself as if for warmth—or comfort. It was somehow a very youthful and oddly moving stance.

She shook her head. 'No. I'm not cold.' She turned to look at him, proud. 'You don't know much about women, do you?' It was a challenge, carefully light. 'You really thought I'd welcome that kind of honesty, I suppose. In fact, it's about the most offensive thing you could have said. You should have dressed it up a little, Griff, if you really want me as much as you say. Women prefer it that way, you see. I might not have believed a word you said but at least I wouldn't feel so . . . so *cheapened*.' Her voice faltered slightly on the word.

Griff frowned. He'd been so sure that she would appreciate and understand his frankness and his reasons for imposing a limit on their involvement. 'I didn't mean to offend you, Kelly,' he said quietly.

'I'm more offended because you didn't even know that you were being offensive. You must think I jump into bed with every man who says he wants me,' she said bitterly. 'Well, you couldn't be more mistaken!'

A couple came out of the house, hand in hand, and looked at them curiously. Kelly took the opportunity to go back to the party. Griff followed her into the house but she eluded any further conversation with him by latching on to Megan and her current boyfriend.

Very shortly, John returned from the pub and came to

find her, sliding an arm about her waist. As she turned, Kelly caught sight of Griff on the other side of the crowded room, talking to some friends. His deep-set and very striking eyes seemed to be resting on her and the anaesthetist with a slightly sardonic gleam of amusement in their depths. She promptly cooled the smile and the welcoming words she'd had ready for John, feeling that the watching surgeon would construe any warmth on her part as a gesture of defiance. She didn't mean to give him the satisfaction of supposing that she was parading her friendship with John just to annoy him. She was determined to show him that she wasn't really interested in any man but Jeremy. Least of all an autocratic and arrogant senior surgeon who thought he had only to crook a finger for a woman to fall into his arms!

He didn't approach her again that evening. She saw him with a number of people and observed the swift reaction of the women to his looks and charm and the light flirtation that was usually bandied about at such parties. He was obviously popular and she wondered if the slight air of reserve made him all the more attractive to women. She'd already discovered that he seldom talked about himself or his personal affairs, but no one could doubt that women played some part in the life of the tall, dark and handsome Griff Rydell.

John took her back to the caravan later that night and forbore to criticise her choice of home. She warmed to him and invited him in for coffee with the confident knowledge that if he made a pass she could keep him at a safe distance. For the first time, she realised that it was easy for a woman to say no and mean it when she wasn't even slightly tempted to say yes. She liked John but there wasn't a scrap of romantic or sexual interest in the way she felt about him. She admitted ruefully that she wouldn't find it so easy to say no to Griff if he persisted in his pursuit. He stirred her too swiftly and too forcefully to feelings such as she'd never known before.

She was annoyed with her response to his smile, his touch, his kiss. She didn't doubt that he'd been aware of it and that was galling. No man ought to be that attractive, she thought crossly. But she didn't have to be fool enough to fall in love with him, she told herself firmly.

She refused to wonder if it was a little too late for caution . . .

Kelly made her way by bus into Penbryn the following morning and found the garage that Griff had mentioned in the High Street. Len Williams was in his tiny office, a burly, good-looking Welshman.

'Yes, I'm Len Williams,' he said in answer to her query, looking her up and down in blatant admiration. 'What can I do for you—and when?'

She smiled. 'I'm Kelly Lorimer. I believe you've agreed to come to my rescue and put new life into my Mini.'

His gaze travelled slowly and lingeringly over her slender figure. 'Now I understand why Griff was so insistent that I should do something about your car. Who wouldn't pull out all the stops for you, darling?' he drawled meaningfully.

Warmth stole into her face at the familiar and flattering words and tone, the way he was looking her over. She wondered if Griff had led him to believe that she was one of his girlfriends. 'He says you're going to work on the Mini over the weekend. That's very good of you, Mr Williams,' she said carefully.

'I'm Len to my friends.' He winked at her. 'Yes. I'll get the lads to go along to where you've left it and bring it down to the garage this morning. Provided it's repairable and I've got the necessary parts, I should have it ready for you by Monday. We're very busy just now and

I wouldn't do this for everyone, mind. But I owe Griff a few favours.'

'I've brought the keys.' She took them from her bag and laid them on the desk.

'It'll be a good job, I promise. And it won't cost you the earth. I've a special price for cars that belong to pretty nurses.'

'How will I know when it's ready? I can leave a telephone number where they'll take a message.'

'I've a better idea, darling. Give me your address and I'll deliver it personally,' he told her with a twinkle in his eyes.

'I don't want to put you to that trouble . . .'

'It won't be any trouble. It might even prove to be a pleasure.' It was mischievous, slightly flirtatious, almost optimistic.

Kelly laughed. Nurses learned in the early days of their hospital training how to cope with amorous males and the burly garage owner was an easily recognisable type. Observing the gold wedding band he wore, she assessed him as a happily married man who liked to flirt a little with a pretty girl but had no real desire to stray. He was just a good-looking, smooth-tongued, slightly conceited charmer who'd probably run a mile if he thought a girl was taking him up on a meaningless suggestion, she thought dryly.

She smiled at him with a deliberate flutter of femininity. 'That would be good of you! What time shall I expect you?'

'Now that's a little difficult to predict,' he prevaricated instantly, backing away from the hint of ready response just as she'd expected. 'I shouldn't be making any promises at this stage, in fact. I haven't had a look at your car yet, have I? Perhaps you'd better give me a call late tomorrow afternoon and I'll let you know how it's

going and when you can expect to be back on the road.
Okay?'

'It certainly sounds a more practical arrangement,'
she agreed. 'I'll do that, Mr Williams.'

As she was in Penbryn, Kelly decided to do some
shopping. Emerging from the small supermarket with a
bulging carrier bag and a lighter purse, she saw Griff on
the opposite pavement, walking towards her. The tall
surgeon in tan slacks and casual shirt drew attention
even without that distinctive hint of lameness. He turned
into a newsagent's shop and she realised that he hadn't
seen her.

She hesitated. She didn't want to make any overtures
that might be misconstrued but she ought to let him
know that she'd called at the garage to confirm the
arrangements he'd made.

She crossed the road, heart bumping against her ribs
with a foolish kind of excitement and anticipation. She
was behaving like a silly schoolgirl with a crush on the
unattainable, she told herself crossly. She reminded
herself that she was no longer seventeen and sighing for
a surgeon who meant to marry her cousin. She was six
years older and wiser, a state registered nurse, mature,
level-headed and worldly-wise—and she ought to know
better than to fancy herself half-way to loving a man
whose only interest in her was blatantly dishonourable.

She waited outside the busy shop, studying the selec-
tion of sweets and toys and fancy goods in the crowded
window, rehearsing how she would greet Griff and what
she would say to him, determined to be just as discouraging as she knew how to be rather than give him the
slightest cause to suspect the way she felt about him or
that she was at all interested in the way he professed to
feel about her.

It was several minutes before he came out of the shop,

returning his wallet to his hip pocket. Seeing Kelly, he paused with no sign of surprise.

'Looking for me?' he asked levelly, the glimmer of a smile in the grey eyes as he looked down at her.

Kelly bridled at the arrogance of the assumption. 'I don't know why you should think that!' she retorted stiffly.

The smile was much more evident as he said lightly, 'So you aren't looking for me. Another blighted hope.'

She threw him a sceptical glance. 'I've just been to the garage.'

'So Len said. You made quite an impression there, you know. I guess it didn't need a word from me, after all. Just one look and he's prepared to work day and night on your car if necessary.'

'Very flattering, but unlikely.'

'You're too modest, Nurse Lorimer.' He softened the formal address into a near-endearment with the deep velvet of his voice. He reached to take the heavy bag of shopping from her hand. 'Come and have some coffee. I live just round the corner, you know.'

'Being grateful to you doesn't have to extend that far, surely?' she demanded very sweetly.

Griff laughed. 'That far but no further, I promise. Unless you want me to have my wicked way with you, of course,' he drawled, eyes dancing with mocking mischief.

Kelly smiled reluctantly, disarmed by the light tone and the reassurance in the way he smiled and put an arm about her shoulders to draw her along the pavement by his side. Just as if they were friends who might very easily turn into lovers, she thought with that familiar tug at her heart as she looked up at his handsome face and then fell obediently into step with him . . .

CHAPTER NINE

KELLY WAS enchanted by the small house of Welsh stone set in a terrace of similar cottages, built almost a century earlier and recently modernised by experts to provide every convenience without spoiling charm and character.

Griff's home seemed to breathe a welcome and a warmth that wasn't entirely due to the money that he'd obviously spent on furnishing it in traditional and comfortable style. Kelly noticed that there was no obvious sign of a woman's influence or possessions and she was strangely comforted to realise that it was very much a bachelor domain.

While he made coffee in the tiny but well-equipped kitchen, she wandered about the sitting-room, studying his books and pictures and record collection, admiring the sophisticated and expensive stereo and video equipment. She was very relaxed. Somehow, it seemed so right and natural that she should be alone with him in the privacy of his home, although she recognised that she'd invited and encouraged a new intimacy with her acceptance of his invitation.

She was her own worst enemy, she admitted frankly, knowing that she would melt at a touch and surrender with scarcely a protest if he attempted to make love to her.

Pride didn't seem to count for anything when it came to loving . . .

She turned with a swift, sweet, slightly shy smile as Griff entered with the coffee things on a tray. It was a smile that had no thought at all for its impact on an unsuspecting man's heart and mind and body, he decided wryly, oddly shaken. He never knew what to expect where Kelly was concerned. Sometimes she was as stiff and defensive and prickly as a hedgehog. At other times, she was all warmth and invitation and encouragement.

The delicate china shivered against itself as he set the tray on a low table and Griff realised that the wave of heady longing that swept through him had unsteadied his hands. Thank God he wasn't operating, he thought dryly, wondering why he wanted her so much when there were plenty of women to provide the kind of satisfaction that had suited his needs for the past six years. He certainly didn't need the complications of serious involvement with a girl like Kelly, he told himself firmly.

There was something special about her attraction for him, however. He liked her pride and her spirit, her touching and very feminine sensitivity. He liked her warmth and sweetness and her impulsive generous nature. She tugged at his heart as well as his senses—and that was the real danger, he admitted ruefully. He was coming too near to needing her for more than a fleeting sexual satisfaction.

For six years, he hadn't felt like loving or trusting any woman. For six years, the desire to keep things light had dictated all his relationships. He'd got over Kate long ago but the memory of her hasty retreat from a disabled fiancé still influenced his thinking and his attitudes.

He sat down and began to pour the coffee into the cups. Outwardly he was confident and very much in control of the situation. Inwardly, he was excited, elated and apprehensive of doing or saying something that would alienate her just when they were on the verge of breaking new and promising ground in their relationship.

'Well, what do you think of my humble abode?' he asked lightly.

'I like it very much. It's—oh, I don't know! It feels like a home,' she said impulsively, sinking into the sofa cushions and smiling at him. 'Nice atmosphere!'

He nodded. 'More than you can say for that ridiculous rabbit hutch of yours, Kelly. Give it up and move in with me.'

The shock of the words caused her hand to jerk and some of the coffee spilled into the saucer. She set down the cup as carefully as she could, heart racing and mouth suddenly dry, not looking at the surgeon. She didn't dare to believe that it was a serious suggestion. It was very much safer to assume that it was light badinage.

'No, thanks. I like my rabbit hutch and I value my independence,' she said lightly.

'You just like living dangerously,' he drawled.

She laughed. 'Probably . . . and I'd miss the cows!' She relaxed against the cushions and looked about the very pleasant room with approval. 'It is nice, though, Griff. Do you look after yourself? Cook and clean and everything?'

'After a fashion. Why do you think I invited you to move in?' Warm humour danced in his eyes.

'I'm not much of a cook,' Kelly told him frankly.

'I dare say your other accomplishments make up for lack of culinary talent,' he said lazily, his gaze moving slowly and meaningfully over the lines of her shapely figure.

Kelly tugged at the skirt of her yellow cotton frock that had somehow ridden up to reveal too much of her slender legs. 'Any time you want an appendix removed or a fevered brow soothed, just call on me,' she agreed flippantly, as though she didn't know exactly the kind of accomplishment he'd had in mind. 'And I'm a dab hand at making beds with perfect hospital corners!'

'There are more things to do with a bed than make it to a ward sister's satisfaction,' he said softly, mischievously, and watched the delicate colour storm into her lovely face. He laughed at her gently, without mockery or malice. 'You blush beautifully.'

'It's the bane of my life,' she said with feeling. She smiled at him wryly.

'I like it. I don't know many girls who can still blush when bed is mentioned.' He leaned forward and reached for one of her slender hands. 'I was very clumsy last night, Kelly. I meant what I said to you, but I said it all wrong. I didn't mean to make you feel cheap. It isn't like that, believe me.'

She looked down at the strong, muscular surgeon's hand that clasped her own, blinking back the tears that the quiet words evoked without warning. She wanted him to *love* her! To *need* her as she was beginning to need him! For ever and always.

It wasn't enough to be wanted for the brief satisfaction of the senses, even if she did realise for the first time in her life that mutual desire was a very powerful and demanding force that was ready to sweep aside every other consideration. His touch transmitted some of his longing and instant response quickened in the depths of her being. A quiver of excitement shafted along her spine. She felt a tingling in her breasts and an ache in her loins. A melting warmth stole through her veins and it took all her strength of will to keep from him the readiness to sink into his ardent embrace.

'Kelly . . . ?'

She shook her head in answer to the urgency in the way he said her name. She drew her hand away from that disturbing touch. 'You only want me because I remind you of Kate,' she said quietly.

'That isn't true, you know,' he told her after a stunned moment.

'I think it is.'

'I'm not looking for a substitute for Kate after all these years.' It was impatient. 'And you aren't so very like her . . . something in your smile, perhaps. A look in your eyes or an inflection in your voice occasionally, that's all! Very little, really.'

Kelly felt that it was more than enough. For every time she glanced or smiled or spoke, he would remember Kate and she just couldn't compete with the cousin who he probably still loved. There was no future in wanting him and only heartache if she allowed herself to love him.

'Making love to me would be like making love to Kate all over again, wouldn't it? But as long as you can keep love out of it then there's no risk that you'll get hurt again, is there?' She was amazed that she could be so cool, so matter of fact, about something that tore her to pieces even to consider. And she was astonished that she could actually smile at him as she spoke.

Griff raised an eyebrow. 'That would be very perceptive if it held even a grain of truth,' he drawled.

'I think it does,' she said with the obstinacy that her family and friends knew so well.

He shook his dark head. 'You're wrong, Kelly. I want you for very different reasons. Kate belongs to the past. I stopped loving her years ago. As far as I'm concerned, it's you and me who matter. Today—and maybe even tomorrow.'

She wished she could believe him. 'No. There isn't any you and me, Griff. Not today or tomorrow.' She was fighting to safeguard her heart even more than the virginity that he threatened with his physical magnetism and her own instinctive response to it.

Abruptly, he rose and reached for her almost angrily, drawing her up and into strong arms so swiftly that she scarcely had time or breath to protest. 'I want you,' he said, low and determined. 'And I *will* have you!'

His mouth came down hard on her own, blotting out everything but a whirling, swirling and very sensuous excitement that leaped in her loins and trembled in her heart.

His kiss was long and deep and demanding. Kelly was breathless and tremulous when he finally lifted his dark head. She'd never known anything like the readiness to give herself utterly to the wonder and enchantment of his lovemaking. She was filled with an intensity of longing to cross the last threshold between virginity and *knowing*. She was twenty-three and a virgin and she didn't know what lay on the other side of surrender— and she wanted more than anything in the world to find out in this man's arms.

With a tremendous effort of will, she put both hands to his chest in a fluttering gesture of defence and thrust him away. 'No!' she said desperately, horrified by that threat of wanton abandon to his need and her own disturbing sensuality.

'Are you trying to tell me that you don't want me, too?'

'That's right!'

He smiled down at her with understanding, a hint of tenderness. 'Do you think I don't know how you quicken when I kiss you?' he said softly. 'Your tongue can lie all it wants but I can taste the truth on your lips.'

His deep voice held all the poetry and all the persuasion of his Welsh blood, and Kelly seemed to have no defence against the velvet of the words, the glow in his grey eyes, the warmth of that smile. Fortunately, her level head wasn't so easily overwhelmed by the dream and the desire that he could evoke so swiftly in her foolish heart and even more foolish body.

'The truth is that I came to Porthbryn to marry Jeremy Hunt,' she declared brightly. And because it was almost true, the words held the ring of conviction. 'I thought you knew. Everyone else does.'

'I'd heard something to that effect. It seemed unlikely,' he said carelessly, thinking of Hunt's affair with Angie Howell, which was common knowledge to everyone but the girl who expected to marry him, apparently. 'I didn't believe it.'

Kelly shrugged. 'Well, you may believe it now,' she told him firmly, convinced that he wouldn't continue to pursue her after that announcement. Now, she only had to make it come true, she thought wryly.

Griff studied the small, pretty face with its stubborn expression and a new kind of dismay struck at the heart that thought it had forgotten how to love. 'I see,' he said slowly, forced to accept the truth of the statement because she had no reason to lie to him.

'So you *did* misunderstand my motives,' Kelly said proudly. 'I haven't been chasing you, as you seem to think. I liked you years ago and I was sorry for you and pleased to see you again and to find how well you've coped with everything that happened. Just friendly interest, that's all. I'm sorry if you thought it was anything else. If I gave the wrong impression . . .'

'Maybe you do mean to marry Hunt. But you'd be in bed with me in ten minutes if I really put my mind to it,' he told her curtly. 'Friendly interest be damned, Kelly! One touch and you're on fire!'

He was too knowing, too direct. Her face flamed.

'Then do me a favour and don't touch me,' she said,

low and angry, resenting his awareness of feelings that a woman prefers to keep a secret. 'I can't help what you do to me, Griff. It doesn't mean that I like it! And I hate you for knowing and saying so,' she added suddenly, very bitterly.

He smiled at her in warm and tender understanding. 'Oh, Kelly, you're very sweet,' he said gently, moved by that impulsive honesty. He stretched out his hand to her and then let it drop as she involuntarily flinched from the threat of his touch. 'All right. I'll make it easy for you. I'll leave you alone. But don't think it will be easy for me, will you?' His voice was ragged with desire and disappointment.

'I think I'd better go.'

'As if we'd quarrelled?' Griff shook his head. 'You don't want us to be lovers but surely we can be friends? So stay a little longer and I'll make some fresh coffee. I give you my word that I won't say or do anything that you don't like.'

She might trust him to keep that promise but Kelly doubted if she could trust herself to remain with this very attractive and increasingly dear man. There was too much temptation to hold out her arms to him and disregard the consequences, she thought wryly.

'I've things to do,' she said carefully.

'What's so important that you have to rush away?'

'I'm meeting Jeremy.' If it hadn't been true, she'd have invented the appointment. As it was, she'd brought it forward by several hours.

'Then I mustn't make you late, of course. I'll take you home.' He looked at her levelly. 'When are you and Hunt getting married, by the way? It seems to be something of a secret.'

'I'm not sure. We haven't actually fixed the date. Fairly soon . . .' The words tumbled in some confusion as she met the rather sceptical expression in those grey eyes. She hoped she was convincing. 'It really depends on Jeremy.' More than he knew, she thought wryly.

For Jeremy didn't seem to be interested in marriage with all its commitments and responsibilities. He would prefer her to be a live-in lover rather than a wife, she knew. Perhaps he was wiser than herself in these days of uncertain and short-lived marriages. Perhaps they *should* live together and find out if they were really suited to each other and could make each other happy. But Kelly was old-fashioned enough to want a wedding ring and the emotional security of knowing that a man loved her enough to pay her the compliment of asking her to marry him. She wasn't even sure if Jeremy really loved her at all . . .

She felt ashamed of her doubts when he welcomed her with loving tenderness in his kiss that afternoon. She clung to him, trying to recapture the former feeling for him, trying to quicken with the desire that had leaped so swiftly for another man. She'd held him at bay for so long. Surely it was time to give herself without hesitation and allow his lovemaking to wipe the memory of Griff Rydell from the slate of her troubled heart and mind.

Her response was slightly too fervent. Jeremy held her away from him, a smile of surprise in his very blue eyes.

'What's all this?' he demanded, teasing her gently. 'Guilty conscience?'

Kelly's heart skipped a beat at the words. 'Should I have?' She moved away, shrugging out of the thin cotton anorak and turning to lay it across the back of a chair, wondering if that encounter with Griff Rydell and the way she felt about the surgeon was written all over her for the whole world to read.

'Last night,' he said lightly. 'John Duncan. Gary Wilmot's party. Home in the early hours!'

'Oh . . . !' She laughed on a small surge of relief. She'd almost forgotten the party and the friendly anaesthetist who'd taken her to it. 'You've heard about that.'

'Darling, you're forgetting the grape-vine,' he said dryly. 'Sneeze in theatre and a sister on any ward in the hospital will prescribe a cure for your cold five minutes later! And you *are* supposed to be my girl. People are bound to talk.' He smiled at her suddenly, very warmly. 'How was the party?'

'The same as any other without you. I wish you'd been there,' she said with truth. Things might not have come to a head between herself and Griff if Jeremy had been around to protect her from that kiss in the moonlight and those blunt words, she thought wryly.

'We could have been together. But you were washing your hair—or words to that effect,' he reminded her smoothly.

Kelly coloured, remembering that she'd put him off when he'd suggested that they should meet. 'It wasn't planned. I met John in the car park when I was going home and it was the first I'd heard about a party.'

'You don't have to explain anything, Kelly. That's our arrangement, isn't it? Free agents. No ties.' He had more reason than she to feel guilty, he thought ruefully, remembering how *he'd* spent the evening.

'It's the way it's always been,' she agreed, brushing a strand of long, windswept hair from her face.

'It's the way you've always wanted it.'

'Yes . . .'

The doubtful tone caused Jeremy's eyes to narrow abruptly. He turned her towards him with a light hand on her shoulder, tilting her chin to look into her face. 'Changed your mind?'

He was giving her the opportunity she'd wanted. Kelly

seized it with both hands. 'I'm beginning to feel that I'd like things to be rather more settled, Jeremy,' she said carefully.

'In which way? Do you want to give me the elbow—or move in?' His blue eyes were very intent as he waited for her to reply.

Kelly drew a deep breath. 'I want us to get married,' she plunged. She put her arms about him and felt him stiffen with an instinctive resistance to the suggestion.

'This is so sudden,' he said flippantly.

'Don't joke, Jeremy. I mean it.'

'I'm not a great believer in marriage, you know.' Women never seemed to think of anything but getting married, he thought wryly. Even Angie, the last girl in the world he'd expected to opt for wedding bells.

He kissed her to take the sting from the words and met with so little response that he lifted his auburn head to scan Kelly's expressive face with slightly ironic amusement in his blue eyes.

'I'm sure we could make it work, Jeremy.'

'I'm not sure at all, darling. I don't think you love me enough,' he told her lightly.

'Jeremy!' Kelly jerked out of his arms in convincing indignation. 'How can you say that? Or even think it! Why do you think I came to Porthbryn if not to be with you?'

'But you *aren't* with me,' he pointed out with unassailable logic. 'You're living in that bloody caravan and going out with other men and still keeping me at arm's length. It isn't good enough, Kelly.'

She sank into a chair, frowning. 'That's what really rankles, isn't it?' she said quietly. 'You haven't been able to get me into bed.'

He smiled. 'If you loved me . . .' he began lightly.

'Oh, not that hoary old chestnut!' She sighed. 'There's

a world of difference between loving a man and wanting to go to bed with him.'

'The two things go together, darling. You must be very naive or very innocent if you doubt it.' He crouched beside her chair and took hold of her slim hands. 'I know it's blackmail of the worst kind. I've never used it before. But now you're forcing me into it. If you love me enough to marry me then you love me enough to go to bed with me. Now.'

Kelly looked into the eyes that held so much love and longing and wondered wryly why she was so unmoved when another man's desire had almost swept her beyond all caution.

She would have gone to bed with Griff without an instant's hesitation if he'd spoken one word that held the promise of love, she knew. So what could be wrong about going into Jeremy's familiar arms when she knew that he loved her, even if he was reluctant to commit himself to the finality of marriage?

'Yes,' she said levelly, without emotion. 'All right.' She stood and freed her hands from his clasp. Jeremy straightened and she reached to kiss him, heart racing, body trembling with nervous apprehension rather than the delightful anticipation that Griff's lips and hands and body had evoked in her.

She drew away and walked across the room and into the bedroom. Jeremy followed. Kelly began to unbutton her blouse with fumbling fingers and he watched her for a moment or two with a wry twist to his lips. Then he moved towards her. Kelly smiled at him shakily. He cradled her face in his two hands and kissed her very tenderly.

'Like a lamb to the slaughter,' he said gently. 'That isn't the way I want you, Kelly.' He began to fasten the buttons of her blouse.

She caught at his hands. 'Are you turning me down?' she demanded as lightly as she could.

'No. But I'll wait until we're married.' He stroked the wing of her pale hair. 'Promise me that you'll be rather more enthusiastic on our wedding night . . .' He put his arms about her and held her without passion, resting his cheek against her soft hair. Marriage had never been a part of his plans for the future. But a man could do worse than settle for someone as dear and as delightful as Kelly, he told himself firmly. He'd loved her for a long time, after all. Angie was just a temporary fever in the blood . . .

CHAPTER TEN

ON MONDAY morning, Kelly arrived in Theatres to find the place buzzing with the news of her engagement to Jeremy Hunt. The very efficient grape-vine had been busy over the weekend.

Few of her new friends at the Porthbryn General were surprised, it seemed. Jeremy had talked about her a good deal and with obvious affection before she came to join him at the hospital, and no doubt it had been assumed by everyone that they meant to marry in due course. Kelly was greeted with a flurry of good wishes and some teasing from her fellow nurses in the changing-room as she donned theatre frock and cap and shoes. But she sensed a little restraint that might almost be disapproval in the manner of some of her colleagues.

Angie was in the office when she went along to report, busy with paperwork. She didn't look up immediately and Kelly felt that she was deliberately ignoring her.

'Good morning, Sister,' she said firmly.

Angie laid down her pen. 'So you're getting married, Nurse Lorimer.' Her voice was hard, unfriendly.

'Yes, Sister. Next month.'

'Oh, all in a rush . . .' Angie's gaze travelled slowly and insolently over Kelly's slender figure in quite deliberate assessment of possible pregnancy.

Kelly bit back annoyance. 'Not really. Jeremy and I have been virtually engaged for months,' she said firmly. She knew that she'd scored as she saw the flicker of hurt that crossed the theatre sister's attractive face. Suddenly, inexplicably, she was sorry for her. Angie

123

looked pale—drawn and unhappy, smudges of weariness beneath the glittering dark eyes. 'Are you all right, Angie?' she asked gently, impulsively, her tender heart moving even for a girl she had no reason to like. 'You don't look well . . .'

Angie looked at her with so much hatred that it was a tangible force in the room. 'I'm perfectly well, thank you, Nurse Lorimer,' she said, emphasising the formality with the coldness of her tone. 'You'd better get on. Newly engaged or not, you've no time to waste this morning. We're expecting an emergency from the Baby Unit and your theatre must be ready for it. Just try to keep your mind on your work if that's possible. I suppose even a Hartlake nurse can get carried away by excitement . . .'

Hurrying along to the theatre, Kelly knew that if Angie could put a spoke in her wheel or harm her in some way, she'd do it without a moment's hesitation. There was so much malice and hostility in the way that she looked and spoke. Had she been so involved with Jeremy? Had he unwittingly led her to believe that there was some future in caring for him? Or did Angie just resent losing him to someone she'd regarded as a rival in more ways than one since their first moment of meeting?

Kelly was feeling terribly guilty about the whole business. For she'd forced poor Jeremy into an engagement and talk of wedding plans when it was the last thing he wanted, although he wouldn't hurt and disappoint her or risk losing her by admitting it. They'd been such good friends for such a long time . . . more than friends. She didn't doubt that he loved her dearly and he deserved so much more than the half-hearted loving that seemed to be all she had to give him since she'd met Griff Rydell again and recognised him as the real and lasting love of her life, her destiny

Loving Griff seemed so hopeless that she might just as well marry Jeremy and try to forget the kind of happiness she might have known with another man, she thought heavily.

She was engaged to Jeremy, just as she'd determined when she threw those proud and impulsive words at Griff—and for all the wrong reasons. Just to prove to another man that whatever her lips and body might convey, she wasn't the least bit in love with him. But she was sure that Griff knew the truth and she was dreading the moment of meeting him that morning. For if he'd already heard the news, he might look at her with that sardonic gleam in his grey eyes that seemed to strip the veil of pretended indifference from her all in a moment . . .

For the next half-hour, she was much too busy to think about Griff or Jeremy or Angie or anything but the urgent case that was coming up from the Baby Unit that morning. A three-day-old baby needed an operation to create an opening between part of the small intestine and the sigmoid flexure of the colon. Clearance of a bowel obstruction in such a tiny patient was a delicate and difficult operation and Griff had been called to deal with the emergency although it wasn't one of his operating days.

Kelly was on her way to the linen cupboard for a supply of towels and drapes for the autoclave when he came out of the office. Not knowing that he was already in Theatres, she was unnerved by the unexpected encounter and the colour swept into her small face and out again, betraying the fluster of her emotions.

It seemed that he meant to pass her without a word or a glance. He looked grim and preoccupied. 'Mr Rydell . . . Griff!' she called him involuntarily.

He turned and looked at her with a blaze of anger that

turned the grey eyes to ice-cold steel and her heart trembled at the curl of contempt about the sensual lips.

'Well?' he demanded curtly. 'What is it?'

Dismayed, she fell back on what seemed to be a reasonably safe subject. 'I only wanted to tell you that I'm collecting my Mini this afternoon,' she said, rather lamely.

His glance raked her with icy indifference. 'I'm no longer interested in your car—or you. Neither of you are worth very much.' It was brusque, chilling.

Kelly stared, hazel eyes registering shock and hurt and dismay. Anger was the most revealing of emotions, however, and she suddenly wondered if she'd thrown away a love she might have had by rushing impulsively into wedding plans with another man. She'd had nothing to lose by admitting that she loved and needed Griff, after all—and she might have gained more than she'd ever dared to dream. For maybe he'd been more serious than she knew when he spoke of wanting her and suggested that she should share his house with him!

She realised that he'd only just heard the news. From Angie. 'I *t-told* you about J-Jeremy . . .' she said defensively, floundering on a sea of doubt and confusion.

The slight stammer and the anxiety in the lovely eyes almost broke through the protective shield of his anger. Almost but not quite. For Griff disliked and deplored the game she was playing with too many lives and the announcement of her engagement to Hunt had been a bad blow, although he believed it to be a gesture of defiance.

'Did you tell *him* about me?' he asked grimly.

Kelly blinked. 'There was nothing to tell.'

'Wasn't there?' His tone was mocking. 'What about the torch you've carried for six years for a man who nearly married your cousin? What about your eagerness to make up to me in any way I liked for what Kate did? What about the way you went into my arms only two days ago—and to hell with Hunt and everything else? Someone ought to warn him that Lorimer women are not to be trusted!'

The scorn lashed her like a whip. The arrogant assurance of the challenging words struck at her pride as well as her heart. She trembled with hurt and indignation that he hadn't hesitated to strip her vulnerable emotions of all camouflage and leave them exposed. 'That isn't fair!' she said angrily. 'You've no right . . .'

He ignored her protest, overriding it as he swept on. 'I'm sorry for Hunt if you really mean to marry him. You're no more in love with the poor devil than Kate was in love with me! But what you have you hold—while you want it! That's it, isn't it? Tarred with the same brush, you and your cousin Kate! Spoiled and selfish and greedy, taking all and giving nothing, using people to get what you want without a thought for their feelings!'

Kelly's heart shook suddenly. 'If I've hurt you . . .'

Griff brushed aside the impulsive words with an impatience born of pride. 'You haven't. Leave me out of it. I'm talking about Angie, for one. Do you know what you've done to Angie? Do you care?'

Kelly stared as the low, furious words registered their full impact on her heart and mind. 'Angie . . . ?' So all that anger, all that concern, was for *Angie's* hurt, *Angie's* disappointment! Kelly's own hurt welled anew and more fiercely at the realisation that the theatre sister was more important to Griff Rydell than she had ever been—or ever could be. *She* was just a passing fancy for a sensual man but Angie was so important that he would stand aside and let her find her happiness with another man if she could—and be glad for her sake!

'No. I don't give a damn about Angie,' she said

quietly, defiantly. 'Jeremy was mine before he ever met her and he loves me. And I love him!'

She brushed past the cold-eyed surgeon and fled to the sanctuary of the linen cupboard. Leaning against the wooden shelves, she pressed one hand to her mouth and the other to the ache in her breast, closing her eyes as the pain swelled, threatening to overwhelm her. She felt sick and dizzy and bruised.

He was a pig, a brute! He knew just how to wound to do the most damage! She hated him! He had no right to know that she'd dreamed about him all those years and thrilled at their second meeting and rushed into loving him like an impulsive fool—and even less right to use that knowledge to hurt her, she thought, struggling with the burning, gasping tears.

She could understand and forgive him if he'd been hitting back at her to avenge his own hurt. But he'd punished her because she'd hurt Angie by taking away the man that the theatre sister presumably loved. That was utterly unforgivable.

The door opened and closed behind her. Kelly hastily reached for a pack of linen, blindly, trembling, and knocked several to the floor with her clumsy hands. She gave a little exclamation of dismay.

Griff pulled her roughly into his arms and kissed her savagely, bruising her soft mouth and crushing her breasts against his hard chest. Kelly gave a little whimper of protest and tried to escape that forceful kiss. She thrust ineffectually at the hand that had curved about her breast in arrogant caress.

'Are you mad?' she demanded, finding the strength from somewhere to push him away. 'What are you doing, for heaven's sake! We'll both be out of a job if Angie walks in!'

He blocked her way as she tried to head for the door.

'Angie would be only too pleased to catch you in my arms.' There was a blaze of determination in the piercing, deep-set eyes.

'I expect she would. And she'd use it to her own ends. But it isn't going to happen,' Kelly said tautly. 'Sister Angela Howell isn't going to spoil things for me and Jeremy!'

'If she doesn't, *I* will,' he promised her grimly. 'I'm damned if I'll let you marry Hunt and break Angie's heart!'

Instinctively, Kelly thrust both hands against his chest as he caught her back into his arms. Despite her hurt and her anger and her alarm, her body welcomed the eager passion with which he forced her against the linen shelves and took fierce possession of her unwilling lips. She didn't dare to let him know it and she resisted him with all her might, body stiff with defiance, mouth refusing to warm to those eager, seeking lips. She thrust a hand through the dark curls on the nape of his neck and tugged to hurt. His head jerked up angrily.

'Don't use me!' she said fiercely. 'I won't be used in this way! You can't change anything, no matter what you do! I'm going to marry Jeremy and I don't care about you or Angie or anybody else!'

'Bitch . . .' He buried his lips in the soft, sweetly-scented hair that had tumbled about her shoulders when the theatre cap slipped to the floor. His body was suddenly hard against her, throbbing. 'Stupid, senseless, beautiful bitch . . .' The groan of longing and the soft murmur of his voice turned every word of abuse into endearment.

The flame of his passion seared her from head to foot. The delicious, frightening fire crept slowly along her veins and she was so weak with wanting that only his strong arms about her prevented her from falling. But she throbbed with love as much as the longing which he had evoked so swiftly and so powerfully in her slender frame. There wasn't even the hint of love in the way he held her and kissed her and crushed her to him on a tidal wave of desire.

A little sob rose in her throat. Hearing it, Griff was suddenly still. He sighed, hot and heavy and despairing.

'Let me go! Oh, let me go,' she said with tears in her voice. Her body ached and tingled and trembled but her heart felt as if it was breaking. 'I hate you!'

He moved away from her, fighting for control. He stooped to pick up her theatre cap and crushed it in his hands. She snatched it from him and rammed it on to her head and began to thrust her long hair up and into it with shaking fingers.

'Kelly . . .'

'Just go away, go away and leave me alone and never, never speak to me again,' she told him passionately. 'You've done nothing but insult me and cheapen me and make a fool of me ever since I came to this place and I'll never forgive you—*never*!'

Griff looked at her for a moment, a nerve jumping in the lean, bronzed jaw. Then he turned and left her.

Not a moment too soon. For Megan came hurrying to find her, to tell her that the small patient was on his way from the Baby Unit to Theatres.

'And I've just passed Griff Rydell on his way to the changing-room. You'll be pleased to hear that he is operating, Kelly. Shouldn't you be gowned and scrubbed?'

'Yes. I'll be there in a moment, Megan. The place fell in on me,' she said as lightly as she could, glad to hide her face by stooping to pick up plastic packs and restoring them to the shelves.

Her whole world had fallen in on her, in fact, she

thought bleakly, wondering how she was going to sort out the sorry mess of her life. But Theatres followed the tradition of its show business name-sake. The show must go on, come what may! So she must scrub up and don gown and gloves and mask and present herself in the operating-room to act out the role of efficient, impersonal theatre nurse at Griff's side, doing the work she'd been very well trained to do. Eyes and hands and minds and hearts working together to save life and preserve health, private thoughts and feelings temporarily pushed aside, personal differences forgotten . . .

The tiny boy was brought into the theatre and lifted carefully on to the table and positioned for surgery by Kelly's gentle hands. He was such a pathetic scrap of humanity that it wasn't surprising that tears sprang to her eyes or that there was a little choke in her voice as she replied to Griff's formally-phrased and quietly-spoken greeting. He sounded exactly as he always did. He knew as well as she did that tongues would soon wag if either of them allowed personal feelings to break through the cloak of theatre etiquette. At times it could be a very useful cover. Certainly Kelly was very grateful for it that morning. It bridged the yawning chasm between that scene in the linen cupboard and the next time they met outside the operating-room.

While she arranged the last of the drapes that concealed most of the infant's frail body, Griff turned to talk to John Duncan. The anaesthetist was busy with the monitors, cylinders and valves that looked and were so complicated and so essential. He would be holding little Peter's life in his hands throughout the delicate surgery, keeping him under the anaesthetic while he watched for cardiac or respiratory failure, any danger of brain or kidney damage.

Griff moved into position and at a nod from the

anaesthetist and a murmur of assent from Kelly, he took
the scalpel that she held out to him and proceeded to
make the first delicate but sure cut. She watched and
assisted, marvelling at the deftness and the dexterity of
the hands that knew exactly what to do, whether they
were wielding a scalpel or tying a ligature or inserting the
neatest of small sutures. And they were probably just as
expert when it came to holding and caressing a woman
into weak and willing submission and surrender, Kelly
thought wistfully. She jerked her thoughts back to the
matter in hand as she realised that he was waiting for her
to swab.

Griff glanced at her with slightly raised eyebrow that
disapproved of the momentary inattention. She looked
back at him with militant eyes above the surgical mask,
defying him to know with that too-quick, too-clever
perception just what had temporarily distracted her
thoughts.

With an air of indifference that effectively dismissed
her slight bristle of indignation, he turned to John.
'How's the little lad doing?'

'He started to cyanose a few moments ago and I
stepped up the oxygen. His colour's improved but I'm
watching him very closely. Will you be much longer,
Griff? We don't want him to start fibrillating at this
stage.' There was a degree of anxiety in the anaesthetist's quiet voice as he warned of the danger of cardiac
arrest.

'Ten minutes, hopefully.'

John checked ventilator and monitor and systolic
pressure gauge. 'That should be okay . . .'

Kelly placed the used swab in a receiver that was
promptly whisked away by Megan. The swab would be
draped on the counting rack with all the rest. Before
Griff began to sew up, every swab and every instrument

would be carefully checked and counted by the theatre team.

Griff stepped back to his position beside the table, flexing cramped hands and blinking eyes that were beginning to ache from concentration on the microscopic surgery. Glancing at him, Kelly saw beads of sweat standing out on his brow and wondered if the long standing was a strain on his still-sensitive spine. It was impossible not to admire his dedication and his determination, although she was still seething at his behaviour.

She took a sterile towel and reached to wipe away the perspiration before it began to trickle into his eyes, careful to keep all expression from her own treacherous face. She was just a nurse doing her job, after all. He thanked her with a curt nod and bent once more over his patient.

Rearranging instruments on the draped trolley, preparing the various sutures and needle-holders that he was likely to need for the delicate task of sewing-up, a pair of scissors slipped through Kelly's gloved fingers.

She bit her lip in annoyance as they hit the floor. She couldn't remember dropping a single instrument in all her years at Hartlake or the months at Marks Cross and it was infuriating that it should happen now. Griff was sure to make some acid comment on her incompetence, she thought, nerving herself. To her surprise, he said nothing. He didn't even glance up, too intent on his task.

'Butterfingers!' It was the anaesthetist who spoke, the light teasing proving that he was not now so tense or so anxious about the tiny boy, who appeared to be standing up well to the final stages of a long and intricate operation.

'Sorry . . .' Kelly's hazel eyes smiled warmly at him

above her mask. John Duncan had been one of the first to wish her happiness that morning and she'd been touched by the warmth and sincerity of the gesture and the instant brushing-away of any disappointment that he might feel on his own part. She knew he liked her. Given time and encouragement, he might have become very fond of her, she felt.

A few minutes later, Griff stood away from his patient and watched while Kelly threaded the nylon suture thread. Conscious of his gaze, she suddenly went to pieces and began to fumble a task that she had performed so many times that it was almost automatic.

'You won't be much use to me or any other surgeon if the thought of getting married affects your head and your hands to such an extent,' he drawled sardonically. 'But I suppose even a Hartlake nurse may be allowed one or two mistakes.'

Kelly knew he referred to personal rather than professional errors and she was immediately on the defensive.

'Hartlake nurses don't make mistakes, Mr Rydell,' she reminded him, light but crisp with pride. 'In or out of theatre!'

'Just live up to that reputation,' he advised, a challenge in the grey eyes. 'We make a good team, Nurse Lorimer. I'd like to keep it that way.'

The smooth words were double-edged. Kelly's heart gave a little jump but she knew it would be the worst mistake she could make to believe anything he said or did in the coming days. She suspected that he would do what he could to wean her away from Jeremy, simply to clear the way for his beloved Angie to get what she wanted. He already had the advantage of knowing that she responded much too readily to his lovemaking and she felt he would use that knowledge at every opportunity.

Suddenly she had no time to think of anything but emergency action as the monitor unexpectedly went haywire. John instantly began to ventilate the patient with pure oxygen while Megan hurried for the defibrillator and Kelly thrust a hypodermic containing adrenalin into Griff's hand. Having injected the drug, he proceeded with cardiac massage until John told him to stop and stand aside while electric paddles were placed in position over the failed heart and the machine switched on in the attempt to jolt it back to reassuring rhythm.

Fifteen minutes later, they were forced to admit defeat. No surgeon liked to lose a patient in such circumstances. Griff had worked so hard to cure the birth defect in his small patient and it was a cruel blow that all his efforts had been in vain.

Kelly's heart went out to him as she saw the bleakness in his eyes. But death was as familiar as birth to doctors and surgeons and nurses, although it could never be regarded as commonplace, whether on the ward or in the operating theatre, and it was never really acceptable except for the very old or the few newly-born who had no real hold on life because they'd been too ill-equipped by nature to survive.

Everyone was depressed, for surgery was teamwork by a number of skilled and experienced people and they had all been involved with the attempt to cure little Peter. It was part of Kelly's job to forget her own feelings and rally her nurses and get them busy with routine tasks to take their minds off the tragedy.

She wished it was as easy to lift Griff's spirits as he dragged off his gown and mask, threw them into the 'dirty' bin and walked from the room. But a friendly word or a smile might make it seem that she'd forgiven him.

And she hadn't. She never would. For he hadn't only captured her heart and knew it too well. He'd also trampled her pride in the dust . . .

CHAPTER ELEVEN

On HER way to change and go off duty later that afternoon, Kelly glanced through the open door of the surgeons' sitting-room in an unconscious search of Griff. She hadn't seen him since he'd walked out of the theatre earlier in the day. She knew he had been involved with the routine procedure and formalities that followed the death of his patient in such unhappy circumstances and another surgeon had taken over his list.

But Jeremy was the only occupant of the room at that moment. As duty surgeon, he was responsible for any emergencies that came in for the rest of the day as well as during the night. They had both been too busy to exchange more than a brief word and a smile since he'd come on duty a few hours earlier.

He was sitting at a table, ostensibly reading the *Lancet*, but he looked so downcast that Kelly doubted if his mind was on the medical journal. She wondered if he was as troubled and doubtful as herself about their precipitated wedding plans and if he would admit it or drift into marrying her because he thought it was what she wanted.

It was possible for a man to be *too* good-natured, she thought wryly . . . and a woman could be an awful fool when she was forced to let pride take precedence over the promptings of her heart. But who could blame her for snatching at the comfort and consolation of Jeremy's declared love for her when there didn't seem to be the slightest hope of any real happiness with a man who hurt and humiliated her at every turn?

With a glance up and down the quiet corridor before entering, for the room was supposedly out of bounds to nurses, she went to Jeremy and bent to drop a light kiss on his cheek. 'Hallo, darling . . .' Gesture and words were warm with her long and genuine affection for him and she hoped it might pass for loving.

He looked up with a smile that seemed slightly forced. 'I'm not sure if that's officially approved behaviour for a theatre nurse. I hope you don't kiss every surgeon you meet in the course of your work, Nurse Lorimer,' he said, mockingly stern.

'Only those who look as if they need it,' she returned lightly.

The gentle probing of the words seemed to pass over his head, unnoticed. 'Then I hope you spared a few for Griff Rydell this morning. I should think he needed cheering up! Angie has just been telling me what happened. Depressing business! We all dread that kind of thing but it's a lucky surgeon who doesn't have it happen to him at some time in his career, I suppose.'

So he'd already talked to the theatre sister, Kelly thought swiftly, forgetting to blush or to feel uncomfortable at that casual reference to the man he must never know that she loved with all her heart. She wondered if Angie had vented some of her apparent hurt on Jeremy and demanded an explanation for his unexpected engagement. She wondered if Angie was entitled to an explanation. Everyone but herself seemed to know just what had gone on between Jeremy and the attractive brunette in the weeks prior to her arrival at the Porthbryn General, Kelly thought dryly—and it seemed that the well-liked theatre sister had some sympathisers. Had Jeremy made an obvious play and some rash promises, or had Angie simply exaggerated a casual interest out of all proportion because she'd fallen in love? Kelly felt *she* could sympathise with such wishful thinking, too!

'Griff Rydell doesn't need me to sympathise or cheer him up,' she said carefully, wondering how Jeremy would react if he knew of the kisses that his fellow surgeon had forced on her in the linen cupboard. 'He's used to coping with set-backs and disappointments. Losing a patient must seem a minor blow after some of the things he's been through.'

'And you wouldn't touch him with a barge-pole, anyway,' Jeremy finished for her, smiling. 'I'd forgotten that you don't like him.' It didn't occur to him to wonder how she knew so much about experiences that the surgeon was reluctant to talk about at any time. 'What kind of day did you have apart from that unhappy affair? Lots of excitement and good wishes and eager questions, I suppose? I'm rather grateful that I missed the first onslaught. I know what nurses are like when it comes to weddings! And I gather that our plans were all over Porthbryn almost before we knew them ourselves?' He shook his head ruefully. 'It's amazing how these things get about!'

'We didn't mean it to be a secret, did we? I think most people are pleased for us, Jeremy. But I did notice a slight frost in some quarters.' Her smile invited him to mention a brief and meaningless involvement with a theatre sister who'd made far too much of the affair. She didn't want to believe that he'd deliberately lied to Angie Howell or misled her with an ulterior motive in mind.

He was suddenly wary and slightly on the defensive. 'Oh, you know me, darling. The great lover! A trail of broken hearts in the four corners of the world!' he declared with not very convincing flippancy. He shut the magazine, pushed it across the table and got up from his chair in one swift movement.

'You may have left one or two nearer home,' she told him dryly. 'You never did seem to know how much damage you do with that devastating charm, Jeremy.' It was light but pointed.

'It doesn't always get me what I want, though,' he returned promptly, sliding an arm about her waist and smiling down at her with a disarming twinkle in his blue eyes. 'It hasn't been very effective where you're concerned, for instance, my love. I'm forced to put a ring on your finger!'

Kelly wasn't so easily distracted and she didn't smile. The teasing words were too near the painful truth.

'Not every girl is as old-fashioned as I am about these things,' she said levelly. She looked up at him with a faint challenge in her hazel eyes. 'I'm wondering if saying no to you for so long made you look round for someone who'd say yes when you left Marks Cross.'

Jeremy still smiled but there was a guarded expression in his eyes. 'Perhaps I did, once or twice,' he admitted with engaging candour. 'A man gets lonely in a strange place and I missed you very much, Kelly. But it didn't mean anything, believe me. It didn't change the way I've always felt about you. You're special.' He bent his red-gold head to kiss her with warm lips.

She drew back slightly. 'Did Angie know that?'

'Angie . . . !' His eyes narrowed, darkened. Then he laughed wryly. 'I'd forgotten the grape-vine. Of course you'll have heard that I took her out a few times.' He wondered if that was the explanation for Kelly's sudden desire to stake her claim to him in the only way that seemed to matter to a woman. 'You don't have to worry about Angie, darling,' he said gently, reassuringly. 'She always knew about you.'

'I wish I'd known about her,' Kelly said dryly, feeling a twinge of sympathy for the woman who'd apparently had good reason to dislike her even before she set foot in the Porthbryn General.

A woman in love needed to believe that a man's pursuit held the promise of loving rather than mere sexual interest. No doubt Angie had clung to that belief where Jeremy was concerned and convinced herself that a distant rival was no rival at all. Now, with Kelly's arrival in Porthbryn followed so swiftly by the announcement of their engagement, it wasn't surprising that she was so dismayed and so bitter.

'Does it make a difference?' he asked carefully.

Kelly hesitated. She didn't want to marry a man who had even the smallest doubt about his love for her. She'd forced Jeremy into an engagement although he'd behaved so beautifully ever since that she was almost convinced that it was what he'd wanted all the time. She knew she must resist the temptation to use a possibly unimportant attachment to another woman to extricate herself. They'd always been honest with each other. She only had to tell Jeremy that she was in love with Griff Rydell and he would instantly set her free.

Somehow, she couldn't put it into words. Voicing her feelings would make them too vulnerable. And maybe she'd lived with a dream of love for so long that she hesitated to turn it into reality. Besides, the admission wouldn't win her the man she wanted and might only hurt deeply the man who declared that he loved her, she thought heavily.

So she said brightly, 'Of course not. After all, it's *me* you're marrying . . .'

'Greater love hath no man,' Jeremy said with an air of supreme sacrifice, smiling. 'If that doesn't convince you that you're the only girl I want, then I don't know what will!' But his heart wasn't as light as the words and he felt like a traitor to truth as he put his arms about her and drew her close.

So did Kelly as she lifted her face to be kissed and tried not to feel that she was plunging even deeper into the pit of her own making . . .

For some days she struggled to come to terms with the thought of spending the rest of her life with someone who was very dear to her but not the man she loved. She found it a tremendous effort to appear the blissfully happy, newly-engaged girl that she was supposed to be, for she dreaded the prospect of marrying one man when her heart sighed so persistently for another.

She avoided Griff as much as possible, thankful that through chance or Angie's design they didn't work together again that week. He seemed to be avoiding her, too. So much for his claim that he wouldn't allow her to marry Jeremy, she thought bitterly. He wasn't making the slightest attempt to win her, by fair or foul means. He was all empty words and indifference—and she was much too proud to show that she minded. Proud and stubborn, just as he declared.

At the end of a day in Theatres that hadn't been heightened for her by even a glimpse of the tall, dark and too-attractive surgeon, she found him waiting for her when she reached the caravan. He sat on the rickety wooden steps wearing jeans and sweater, for it was a chilly and overcast evening, watching her approach with an enigmatic gleam in the deep-set grey eyes.

At the sight of him, Kelly's step faltered and her heart gave such a bound that it nearly flew over the distant hills. She didn't know what to make of his unexpected presence at the caravan but she couldn't believe that there was pleasure in store for her as she saw his grim expression.

'What are you doing here?' She didn't know whether to smile or not. Her heart longed to welcome him but her pride was rearing on its hind legs to protect her from further hurt and humiliation.

'I've had a letter from Kate,' he said without preliminary. It was angry accusation.

'Oh . . . !' Kelly's face was suddenly suffused with guilt. With a date for the wedding tentatively fixed, she'd felt obliged to write and tell family and friends of her plans to marry Jeremy—a man they'd met and liked when he was at Marks Cross.

Somehow, a mention of Griff had crept into her note to Kate. Perhaps she'd been too impulsive, as usual, but it had seemed only right that her cousin should know that he'd recovered from the several blows he'd suffered six years before. Kelly had sincerely felt that it would relieve a mind that must occasionally be troubled by a sense of guilt.

'You told her that I was here.'

'Yes. I'm afraid I did.'

'I'm obliged to you,' he said, so coldly that it chilled her heart. 'She wrote care of the hospital and it was handed to me this afternoon. Do you know how I felt about that?'

'I can imagine.' It was low-voiced, contrite.

'I doubt it. Imagination doesn't seem to be your strong point,' he said brutally. 'Damn you, Kelly!'

Understanding, she forgave the violence. She fumbled with the key to the caravan. 'I think you'd better come in, Griff. I'll make some . . .' She broke off, biting her lip, colour flooding her small face.

'Tea and sympathy!' It was cutting. 'I've never known anyone as stubborn as you! Get an idea into that head of yours and nothing can shift it, and I think you'd rather die than admit to being wrong about anything!'

Kelly didn't answer. Brushing past him, she inserted the key in the lock and opened the flimsy door. Griff rose to his feet and followed her into the caravan, looking about him with obvious disapproval of its shabby furnishings and peeling paintwork and limited amenities.

'Make yourself at home,' Kelly said, rather stiffly, taking off her anorak and hanging it up inside a tiny cupboard that did service as a wardrobe.

Griff sat down on the edge of the narrow bunk, testing it for comfort. 'My God!' he exclaimed dryly. 'Do you wear a hair-shirt, too?'

Kelly didn't mean to smile at the sardonic words but her lips quirked just a little, for all the turmoil of heart and mind and body at this unexpected encounter with a man she wished she didn't love. 'It isn't so bad,' she defended.

'Well, I wouldn't want to spend my nights on it. Not even with you,' he told her bluntly.

Not wishing to enter into those dangerous realms, she hastily reached for the kettle and filled it from the tap and set it on the small and not very efficient gas ring.

'That looks as if it might blow us both to kingdom come,' he commented.

'It won't.' She turned to look at him levelly. 'Am I allowed to know what Kate said in her letter?' It was strange how the link with Kate had bound them from the beginning and still continued to do so, despite everything. Knowing him all those years ago had made it impossible for her to think of him as anything but a friend at their first meeting—and loving him had been too easy because the foundations had been laid when she first knew him.

Griff took the letter from his trouser pocket and

tossed it across to her, unsmiling. Kelly caught it and drew out the thin sheet of notepaper covered with the familiar script. But she didn't have time to read it before he spoke.

'She's glad to hear that I'm well and working again and that everything has turned out so marvellously for me. Reading between the lines, she's wondering if she did the wrong thing when she dropped me like a hot brick.' It was cool, sardonic. 'You said she was happy with her engineer.'

'So she is . . . so I thought.' Kelly floundered, dismayed. She drew a deep breath. 'I'm sorry, Griff. I didn't dream that she'd write to you.' But she ought to have known, she realised ruefully. Impulsive behaviour was a family trait.

She realised it was impossible for him to forgive and she didn't blame him for being angry, however well-meaning her mention of his recovery or Kate's letter. It seemed that he really had got over loving Kate. But as his affections seemed to be centred on Angie Howell these days it was just as hopeless for *her* to want him, Kelly thought unhappily.

'Women never accept the end of anything unless it happens to suit them. Women like Kate never believe that any man can stop loving and needing them, I'm afraid. While she thought I was tied to a wheelchair for life, she wasn't interested or concerned. Now, she thinks that she may have opted for second best, after all.'

'She doesn't say that!' Horrified, Kelly glanced down at the letter and scanned it hastily. But it seemed to be a very ordinary note filled with friendly interest and good wishes. Such as she might have written herself in similar circumstances, she decided loyally.

'Not in so many words,' he agreed dryly.

She looked at him doubtfully. 'I'm sure that you're wrong . . .'

'I'm sure I'm right.' It was grim.

'Well, I'm sorry,' Kelly said again, rather lamely. 'I just felt she would be pleased . . .'

'I wonder what you said in your letter to Kate?' he drawled, eyes intent on her flushed face. 'What is it she writes? *Glad to hear that you and Kelly are such friends. I'd like to think that she reminds you of me just a little . . .*'

The colour deepened in Kelly's face and she rushed into speech. 'I could scarcely tell her that you hate me for reminding you of her!' She didn't realise the betraying wryness of the words.

'Is that what you think?'

'That's how it is, isn't it?'

He shook his head at her in amused reproach. 'Such wild exaggeration. Typical feminine behaviour! I don't hate you at all, Kelly. I'm extremely annoyed with you, though. Oh, not for writing to Kate. That's unimportant, although I could have done without hearing from her again, now or ever. I'm very cross about this stupid business with Hunt,' he said bluntly.

Kelly bridled instantly at the implication that he had the least right to be annoyed about anything she did. 'It isn't stupid. I'm going to marry Jeremy.'

'I said you were stubborn.'

Unexpectedly, Griff put out a hand and drew her towards him, decisively. Kelly tried to resist but his grip was powerful enough to hurt and he was much too strong for her to challenge him without losing her dignity.

'Don't start anything!' she warned unsteadily, stiff with pride and determination to keep him at bay. Still sitting on the bunk, his too-attractive face was on a level with her own. She couldn't analyse the expression in his narrowed eyes but her heart was leaping like a wild thing in her breast.

He smiled. 'I'm planning to finish something,' he told her coolly. 'But first I want the answer to a few questions.'

Kelly's chin went up at the peremptory tone and manner. 'You probably haven't the right to ask any of them!'

He shrugged. 'As a doctor, I've been trained in preventive medicine,' he drawled with a flicker of a smile in the grey eyes. 'And I think you both need a dose of strong common sense.'

'And I think you should mind your own business,' she said tartly.

'Do you love him, Kelly?'

It was very direct, taking her breath away. She couldn't answer him. For she would have had to lie and somehow she couldn't bring herself to do that. Even pride couldn't compel her to betray the throb of love and longing in the depth of her being for the man who challenged her so bluntly.

She chose to say nothing and let him think what he would. She looked over his dark head, through the small window of the caravan at the grazing cows at the far end of the field, and felt the silence weighing heavily between them. Her heart was beating very fast, high in her throat, and she was much too conscious of the strong hand that held her so firmly by the wrist and her nearness to him.

He waited and she was tense, sensing the force of his personality and knowing that he was willing her to meet his eyes, to answer him in the way he wished. She resisted with all her might.

At last he spoke again. 'Do you think he loves you?'

It was quiet, unexpectedly gentle, warm with understanding.

Kelly looked at him then, defiant. 'Yes,' she said firmly. 'I know he does.'

She stifled her doubts rather than allow Griff to suspect them. She felt he would seize on the least hint of hesitancy to point out that she should free Jeremy from their engagement and give him time to make up his mind which woman he really wanted. He was still so concerned with Angie and her feelings and her future, Kelly thought bleakly. She felt he would use any weapons to secure Angie's happiness—and too bad if he shattered *her* hopes and dreams and plans in the process! For he couldn't know that she wasn't very much in love with Jeremy.

A smile hovered about the sensual mouth. 'Pair of fools. Why can't you be honest with each other?' It was indulgent rather than impatient. He put his hands on her slim waist and held her lightly, keeping her close and captive without really trying. 'He isn't the right man for you, Kelly,' he said quietly.

'I think I'm the best judge of that!'

Kelly knew she should move away from him as she sensed the stirring of passion that seemed to be transmitted through his strong but surprisingly gentle hands. Desire quivered like a shafting arrow of flame in herself as she quickened to the temptation and the promise in his touch. She tried desperately to cling to sanity and reality but she was fast falling into a dream of the ecstasy to be found in this man's embrace.

'He's weak. You need a man with strength and spirit and integrity to match your own. You need someone as proud and as passionate as yourself. I won't let you throw yourself away on a man who'll never make you happy.' His hands tightened suddenly and fiercely and his voice grew harsh. 'I want you and I *will* have you,' he said throbbingly, as he'd said once before. And he meant it with all the urgency of the need she evoked so swiftly and so fiercely, a need that was so much more than merely sexual, taking him unawares and breaking through all the defences that had protected him from the pain of loving for six years. He rested his dark head on her lovely breast. 'I came here to fight with you,' he said achingly. 'Now, I only want to hold you . . .'

Kelly struggled with the wave of love and longing that stole through her veins, making her weak with wanting and powerless to resist the appeal he was making to her emotions and her senses. 'Don't, please don't,' she said shakily. But her hand moved of its own volition to touch the dark curls in an unmistakably loving gesture and her heart moved abruptly in her breast with all the force of her feeling for him.

She knew it was madness. She knew she might regret it for the rest of her life. But there was too much need in her for the warmth of his lips and the power of his arms and the fire in his embrace.

Impulsively, she moved into him and kissed him on a little sigh of surrender . . .

CHAPTER TWELVE

GRIFF's arms tightened about her and he drew her down to the narrow bunk with him, crushing her with the weight of his hard and urgent body.

Kelly drowned in the deep waters of his kiss and briefly surfaced some moments later to find that he was unfastening the buttons of her thin frock with hands that shook slightly. She made a token murmur of protest that he disregarded, his mouth coming down hard and forceful on her own once more.

Her body melted and she shivered with delight and apprehension as the long, clever hands touched lightly, then lingered and caressed the soft silk of her breasts. His warm mouth strayed from her lips to the slender lines of her neck and down to the hollow of her throat and then slowly but surely to the swell of her breasts. She caught her breath as he hovered, hesitated, and then kissed each in turn, paying homage.

'You're beautiful,' he said softly, with longing.

She wanted him with every fibre of her being. But she was a virgin and afraid. 'I'm not sure I want this to happen,' she said weakly, clinging to him, loving the warmth and the strength and the surprising wealth of tenderness in his embrace.

'*I'm* sure,' he declared forcefully and there was the warmth of reassurance in the way he smiled into her hazel eyes. 'Trust me, Kelly. This was meant to be from the moment you came to Porthbryn—and we both know it. We've just been fighting it but the way we feel about each other has to be something rare, something special.

A gift. Take it and enjoy it.' He kissed her, very gently. Then he drew away and rose to pull the thin sweater over his head, revealing the rippling muscles of his bronzed chest and back.

As he turned to strip out of the rest of his clothes, Kelly saw the scars from several operations on his back. Her heart moved with love and compassion and admiration for his determination to overcome disability. She stretched out her hand to stroke his flesh and then moved swiftly to touch her lips to the scarred back, forgetting to feel threatened by his lean and muscular nakedness.

He stiffened and spun, suspecting pity . . . and relaxed as he saw the glow of love in those hazel eyes. He smiled down at her.

'You're very sweet,' he said gently. 'You always were worth a dozen Kates. Meeting you again is one of the best things that's happened to me, Kelly.'

She trembled before the look in his eyes. 'I hope you mean that . . .'

He undressed her slowly, reverently. He kissed her with a tenderness that stilled alarm; his hands rippled across her body in slow caress and she arched, clung, as the leaping desire threatened to overwhelm her utterly.

He made skilful, sensual love to her with his kisses and caresses and murmured endearments, sweeping her slowly but surely towards the ultimate and much-desired surrender and ecstasy. Kelly fell deeper into love with every kiss, every touch, every soft and seductive word and she longed to please and delight him so that he would never want any woman but herself for as long as they both lived.

Jeremy, Angie, Kate . . . everyone and everything else was forgotten but the delight of his nearness as she thrilled to the strength of his arms, the warmth of his flesh beneath her lips, the long, hard lines of his body crushed against her own. She was an incandescent flame of love and longing as she lay in his embrace and knew the beginning of the heaven that man and woman could find in each other's arms.

She twined her fingers in the crisp black curls on the nape of his neck. She traced the line of the scar that ran from temple to jaw with tender touch, filling with compassion for all that he'd suffered, mentally and physically, and resolving to compensate him in any way she could for as long as he wanted her. Words of love that she didn't dare to utter trembled on her lips, surging from a full heart but believing themselves to be totally unwelcome. She refused to mind that he did not and never would love her in return. It was enough that she loved him . . .

Consumed with wanting, Griff found it hard to control the rising tide of his passion but he was anxious to ensure her delight as well as his own. Her response was total, utterly generous. She was so warm and willing and wonderfully loving in his arms that the heart that had vowed never to love or trust any woman again found itself near to relenting and almost owning to a real and lasting need.

Passion surged, fierce and compulsive, suddenly slipping its leash and carrying her with him on the raging tide. Almost before Kelly knew it, their bodies had merged and were moving in glorious and tumultuous unison towards the towering peaks of mutual and ecstatic delight.

When he lay quiet, spent and breathless, his lips still clung and his arms still enfolded her as though he never meant to let her go again. Kelly held him, waiting for the racing of her heart to quieten and the tumbling of her senses to subside, filled with a golden glow of content and a sense of wonder. At last she knew what lay on the other side of surrender and she marvelled at the power and the glory that she'd found in his arms. The power of mutual and magnificent passion and the glory of giving for each other's delight.

The virginity she'd valued so much and guarded so carefully was irrevocably lost to a man who didn't love her at all. Just like her heart. But Kelly couldn't regret that magical, almost mystical initiation by a man who was a perfect lover as much through instinct as experience.

She loved him more than ever. She'd loved him since she was seventeen and the bud of that early love had waited all these years to blossom into full flower with his second advent into her life. Destiny would have its way, come what may!

If she was very patient and understanding and just went on loving without asking anything in return, perhaps one day he would come to love her just a little, she thought wistfully and with the optimism that was so much a part of her nature. Surely two people couldn't share the incredible delight and wonder of such love-making unless they were meant to be together in love and mutual need for the rest of their lives . . .

Griff stirred, reluctant to break the spell of enchantment that bound them both. His lips moved against the warm sweetness of her soft mouth. It was half kiss, half murmured endearment. 'Darling Katy . . .' It was drowsy, unthinking, touched with content.

He didn't even know that he'd called her by another woman's name.

The shock ran the full length of Kelly's spine and quivered in every fibre of her being. If he'd taken a knife and plunged it deep into her heart, the pain couldn't be any worse, she thought numbly, stricken and unbelieving and feeling as though all the breath had been jolted from her slight body.

She'd known all the time, of course.

Even while he held her and kissed her and made tender and tumultuous love to her, she'd known that it was really Kate in his arms rather than herself.

She'd refused to heed common sense and caution. She'd chosen to believe that she could erase the last, lingering memory of her lovely cousin from his mind and heart by going into his arms eagerly and with love. She'd rushed headlong into giving too much too soon and she had only herself to blame that she'd made a complete fool of herself over an attractive charmer of a senior surgeon. For hadn't he told her only too plainly that loving played no part in the way he wanted her, and never would? And hadn't she always known, deep in her heart, that Kate was the only real and lasting love of his life? Even Angie was no true threat, after all . . .

But, worse than anything, she'd betrayed Jeremy's love and trust and endearing patience, she thought heavily, despairing.

Griff raised his dark head and searched her pretty and slightly anxious face, sensing her sudden tensing and the unspoken turmoil of her thoughts and emotions.

'What is it, Kelly? Regrets?' he asked quietly, wryly, feeling that things had happened almost too fast for him and suspecting a little of what was going through her mind. Newly engaged to one man, she'd been swept off her feet by another—and he didn't envy her the task of telling Jeremy Hunt. 'Not hating me, I hope.'

Somehow, she managed to smile. Somehow, she even managed to answer him with natural-sounding ease. 'Nothing's wrong, except that I think the kettle has probably boiled dry!'

He laughed softly, relaxing. 'So I don't get any tea?

Just the sympathy!' Their recent closeness and its golden aftermath encouraged him to tease her gently, to smile into her lovely eyes.

The light words weren't meant to hurt, Kelly knew, but they pierced her breast with fresh pain. 'More than you deserve,' she retorted with admirable lightness. 'When I think of the things you've said and done.'

'I thought you were pleased,' he murmured, low and mischievous.

'Since I came to Porthbryn,' she said firmly, mockingly stern.

'Defence mechanism,' he drawled. 'I knew you were going to become too important.'

It was too light, unconvincing. Kelly didn't feel at all important to him when she thought of the way that he'd murmured *Darling Katy* in her ear only moments after sharing those rapturous heights with her. Her heart swelled once more and she marvelled that she wasn't crumpled in a heap on the floor, hugging her shattered heart and trampled pride, instead of bandying light words with him as though she was an old hand at the game of love.

Slipping from his arms, she reached for his clothes as well as her own. Dropping jeans and sweater on his bronzed and muscular chest, she said, 'Get up and get dressed, for heaven's sake. Think of my reputation. Cows are dreadful gossips, you know.'

She sounded so cool and so matter of fact that Griff wondered if she was more sexually experienced than he'd supposed. She'd made love to him just as expertly and just as sensually as he'd made love to her, after all. He'd thought of her as shy and vulnerable, almost virginal, and he'd found it easy to overlook the importance of Jeremy Hunt in her life, although she'd promised to marry the man. Now, he wondered if his colleague was only one in a line of past lovers for a pretty and enchanting and very appealing girl.

He was suddenly swamped by a tidal wave of jealousy that took him one step further towards admitting that he was in love with a Lorimer for the second time in his life—and so much more this time that to lose Kelly as he'd lost Kate would destroy him completely. She had a warmth and a sweetness and a generosity of spirit that he'd never found in her cousin, for all Kate's beauty and vivacity.

The low pressure of gas had saved the kettle from total destruction. But it wasn't in very good condition when Kelly whisked it from the ancient cooker. Another casualty of Griff Rydell's dangerous charm and overwhelming physical attractions, she thought ruefully.

Griff slid an arm about her shoulders and turned her towards him. 'I'll buy you a new kettle,' he promised, smiling at her expression.

'Don't bother. I won't be needing it,' she said brightly, hands moving instinctively to his chest to ward him off. 'I'm moving out of the caravan this weekend. I'm going to live with Jeremy. There's really no point in paying two lots of rent now that we've decided to get married.'

It was a sudden and very impulsive decision. She'd meant to keep on the caravan until she actually married Jeremy. But now she wondered if she could endure to spend even one more night within four walls that were impregnated with the memory of another man's lovemaking.

His eyes narrowed abruptly. 'Then nothing's changed?'

Kelly smiled at him. 'You're a very attractive man and I'm just a poor weak woman who couldn't resist temptation,' she said quietly. 'But I'm still going to marry Jeremy. You see, I really do love him. Isn't that what you wanted to know?' After all that had happened, she felt she owed it to Jeremy to utter the lie and she hoped it was convincing. She was very careful to keep all hint of defiance or bravado out of her tone.

The quiet words with their seeming frankness were effective. Griff looked down at her for a long moment, his jaw tensing. All expression vanished from the deep-set grey eyes and his sensual mouth quirked with a trace of mockery that was for his own folly rather than her astonishing preference for another man. He was proud and sensitive and he'd lowered his guard to allow this girl into his heart despite all his resolution and all his mistrust of women in general and Lorimer women in particular. It had been a mistake.

'Then he's a very lucky man,' he drawled indifferently. He reached for her hand and lifted it to his lips with a mocking gesture of finality and farewell. 'I hope I know when I'm beaten . . .'

He had won a total victory if only he knew it, Kelly thought bleakly, fighting to keep the tears from spilling as he made his way across the field towards the five-barred gate and the coast road and his car. She longed to run after the tall and beloved figure with that slight drag of the long left leg that caught so fiercely at her tender heart. She wanted to throw her arms about him and confess that she'd lied and declare that he was the only man she would ever want, now and always and forever. Until the end of time.

Instead, she retreated into the caravan and shut the flimsy door, and the tears that she'd been too proud to let him see began to trickle slowly down her cheeks.

Kelly had to pull herself together in time to get ready to spend the rest of the evening with Jeremy. She was thankful that they'd arranged to go to a club with some friends. She hoped she could hide the obvious low of her spirits from him and it might best be achieved in the company of other people. Alone with him, faced with his tender and patient and very considerate lovemaking, she wasn't sure that she could trust herself not to blurt out the truth about herself and Griff with all her usual impulsiveness and her natural hatred of deceit and lies.

She stared at her reflection in the spotted mirror when she was ready and waiting for the familiar toot of his car horn, wearing the dark blue silk frock that Jeremy liked and her hair in a cluster of curls tied with a matching ribbon, and wondered if she looked any different. She felt that she *ought* to look like a girl who'd crossed the most important threshold of her life in the arms of the man she loved. She was grateful that she seemed to look much the same as usual. A little flushed, perhaps, eyes rather too bright, mouth swollen and tremulous from Griff's exciting kisses, but otherwise no different. Outwardly . . .

She turned to look around the caravan and suddenly decided that both Jeremy and Griff were right about its unsuitability. She had known within a few days that it was shabby and squalid and inconvenient but she had been too stubborn to admit to her mistake. Now, she also admitted that she was far too vulnerable, living by herself in a field on the outskirts of the town.

Griff had apparently climbed over the gate and strolled across the field to sit on the caravan steps for some time before she arrived without being challenged by the farmer or his wife, and it could easily have been a stranger waiting for her in the dusk of the evening, Kelly thought with a little shiver of fear.

She would move in with Jeremy as soon as possible, just as he'd wanted since she'd arrived in Porthbryn. She *was* going to marry him, if only because there didn't seem to be anything else for her now. Griff didn't love her at all and she had finally accepted that it was utterly hopeless to try to compete with the memory of Kate. But Jeremy loved her. She clung to that belief and that comfort—and clung to him, too, when he turned to kiss her as she got into the car.

He drew back and looked intently into her face. 'Did I do something right?'

'Right?' She was puzzled.

'That's a very warm welcome.'

'Oh!' Kelly smiled at him, warm with affection and contrition, even more determined that he must never know that she'd gone into another man's arms so readily and so generously, giving what she'd always denied him so resolutely. 'I'm just glad to see you.'

Jeremy felt slightly uneasy. He'd always liked and welcomed her light touch, her lack of intensity, her few demands. Their relationship had always been so easy and comfortable, untroubled by misunderstandings or imagined slights or small jealousies—or any hint of possessiveness on either side.

Friends more than lovers, they'd both been free to enjoy the company of other people while choosing to spend much of their time together. Unlike other girls, Kelly had never tried to tie him down or force him to commit himself to a lasting bond. And he'd respected her insistence on staying a virgin and admired her for it. She'd been admirably suited to the role of steady girlfriend for a surgeon who was far from ready to contemplate marriage.

Until she'd arrived in Porthbryn.

Perhaps she'd been encouraged, by his letters and telephone calls and his genuine wish to have her working at the same hospital, to believe that he loved and needed her more than he'd ever admitted. Or maybe she'd learned about Angie and discovered that she loved him too much to lose him to another woman, he thought wryly. But her attitudes had certainly changed.

Suddenly, she was all for getting married. Suddenly, she was leaning heavily on him, making demands on his affection and loyalty and time—and his instinctive inclination was to back away. He didn't want to feel that he was so important to her happiness. He didn't want to be that responsible for any woman's emotional security. He didn't want the weight of responsibility for a wife and a mortgage and possible children, and he was rapidly regretting the weakness that had brought about their engagement.

Besides, he'd hurt Angie and that bothered him. Jeremy wasn't the kind to want to hurt anyone and he felt particularly bad about hurting Angie. She'd trusted him. They'd been very close and he liked her a lot. He owed her a lot. He was already missing her a lot, too, he admitted wryly. Kelly was a lovely girl and he loved her and it was impossible to let her down. But there was something about Angie . . .

Turning the car, he headed towards the town. 'It's a rough night,' he commented, increasing the speed of the wipers to cope with the streaming torrent of rain that was being swept in from the sea by the strong wind. The car was buffeted by sudden gusts as they drove along the high and exposed coast road. 'I won't be too happy about leaving you in that caravan tonight. You'll probably wake up in the morning and find you've been whisked out to sea by this gale!'

It was the opening that Kelly needed. 'The weather hasn't been very kind this week,' she agreed. 'And the forecast isn't good. The wind howling round the van kept me awake for ages last night. I'm rather tempted to take you up on your original invitation and move in with you.'

'As lodger or lover?' He glanced at her with a smile that concealed surprise and the light words that he knew she would expect from him.

She tucked her hand into his arm. 'Any way you want me,' she said rashly.

'That sounds like an offer I can't refuse.' It was slightly forced. Jeremy felt as if very deep waters were slowly closing over his head and he suddenly knew that the sweet and lovely and virginal Kelly was the last woman he really wanted in his flat and in his arms and in his life for always. He'd made a mistake. It seemed much too late to say so.

'Then I'll tell Mrs Evans tomorrow that I'll be giving up the caravan earlier than expected,' Kelly said brightly, unaware that she struck fresh dismay into his heart with the words.

'Fine. When are you thinking of moving in?' It seemed that she'd made up her mind in advance and he tried hard to sound enthusiastic. Wasn't she doing exactly what he'd asked of her in the first place? So why did he feel that his precious freedom was slipping away from him—and for all the wrong reasons? For the wrong woman, he amended with a sudden rush of insight, knowing that he wouldn't mind so much if he was giving it up for Angie . . .

'The weekend?' Kelly suggested, burning her boats.

'This weekend?'

It was slightly too quick. Kelly smiled at him, believing she understood that hint of dismay. Poor Jeremy. He'd expected to have a little longer to think about it before he was committed to a whole new way of life. 'Not convenient?'

'You've forgotten my trip with Steve and Mike,' he said carefully, referring to a rock-climbing expedition with some friends that had been planned for some time.

When he'd told Kelly about the arrangement, she'd agreed that he should honour it. He'd been inclined to put it off but now he welcomed the thought of a few days in the Welsh mountains and time to come to terms with his mixed-up feelings. It was obvious that he had to make up his mind which woman he wanted and make it clear to both before he found himself married to Kelly, willy-nilly!

'Oh, of course! You must go, Jeremy. I know you've been looking forward to it,' Kelly said instantly, swamped with relief. She was prepared to take the plunge if she must, but she wasn't sorry to postpone it for a few days. 'Next week will do perfectly well.'

'We'll talk about it again when I get back,' he temporized.

Kelly was struck by something in his tone that sounded almost like evasion and then decided that it was wishful thinking.

For it would be too ironic if she was forcing herself on a man who didn't really want her and running away from a man who apparently did . . .

CHAPTER THIRTEEN

'So WE *are* to have the benefit of your company today after all, Nurse Lorimer! I'd quite given up all hope!'

Kelly checked at the snap beneath the dulcet sweetness of the theatre sister's words and looked into the office. She'd hoped to pass the door unnoticed. Not because she minded a well-deserved rebuke for being more than half an hour late on duty, but because she'd caught a glimpse of Griff, standing by the desk, and she didn't feel up to facing him just at that moment.

'I'm sorry I'm late, Sister,' she said formally.

'I dare say you have an excellent excuse?' Angie suggested. 'Come in and tell me about it. You *were* going to report to me, of course?'

'Yes, Sister.' Reluctantly, Kelly entered the room. Griff didn't glance up from the large, stiffened sheet of paper that was spread out on the desk and seemed to be engaging all his attention. 'I'm afraid I overslept, Sister,' she said carefully, standing in front of the desk with hands clasped demurely behind her back in traditionally dutiful stance and feeling like a first-year. Just as Angie intended, no doubt.

She'd had a really bad night, kept awake by torrential rain and gusting wind and the haunting memory of Griff's arms about her and his body close to her own on the narrow bunk bed. She'd finally fallen into a restless sleep only to dream a dreadfully hopeless dream about the surgeon.

Now he was behaving as if she didn't exist any more for him. Had he lost all interest with her declaration that she loved Jeremy and meant to marry him? Or was he struggling to accept that it was all over between them before it had really begun? Or had he only ever wanted one thing and taken it and decided that she was a disappointment for a sensual and sexually experienced man?

The lift of Angie's dark brow implied that it wasn't a very credible explanation. 'Oh?'

'Then my car wouldn't start,' Kelly added for good measure and with perfect truth. She'd had to abandon the Mini and run for a bus. The little car had been much more reliable since its overhaul by Len Williams but it hadn't liked being left out in the open on such a night and she suspected that the cold and the damp had got into the engine. She stole a glance at Griff as she spoke and thought she saw a twitch of amusement about the sensual mouth . . . or was it impatience, she wondered wryly.

'How unfortunate for you,' Angie sympathised without sympathy or warmth. 'You'd better provide yourself with a reliable alarm clock and reliable transport for the next few weeks, Nurse Lorimer. I'm sure you don't want to run the risk of not getting to the church in time. Your bridegroom might get cold feet and change his mind if you keep him waiting at the altar.'

Kelly didn't rise to the obvious bait. 'If he's going to change his mind I think he can be trusted to say so before he gets as far as the altar,' she said lightly.

'You know him better than I do, of course.' Angie's tone was brittle with bitterness. 'You ought to know if he's the type to let a girl down without warning.' She turned to the silent surgeon and drew his attention to a detail on the paper he was studying, and for a few moments they talked in low tones, ignoring Kelly.

She waited for permission to leave and carry on with

her work. A well-trained nurse followed the rules of hospital etiquette no matter what she felt about a sister's offensive attitude or a surgeon's lack of courtesy, she reminded herself firmly.

The conversation seemed to have become intimate and she resisted the temptation to strain her ears but she was sure that she heard Griff say, 'Meet me tonight,' and her heart contracted with jealousy.

A few moments later, he turned to the door. 'I may be a little late but I *will* make it, Angie. That's a promise. Seven-thirty, did you say?'

Angie folded the stiff sheet that seemed to be some kind of architectural drawing. Kelly suspected that it had been the theatre sister's excuse for calling the surgeon into her office. 'I knew I could rely on you.' Smile and voice held the warmth of affection and long association. As Griff went from the room with the merest nod for the patient Kelly, Angie's glance fell on her with dislike in the depths of her dark eyes.

'Oh, you may go,' she said coolly, dismissively. 'Try not to make a habit of sleeping late.'

Kelly was too sick at heart to bridle at the injustice of the remark. 'Very well, Sister.' It was the entirely automatic response of a well-trained nurse to a senior's admonishing tone. She turned to leave, wondering bleakly how Griff could arrange a date with another woman in her hearing and then nod to her so indifferently, without even the flicker of a smile on his way from the room. Was she so unimportant to him? And she'd spent the best part of the night worrying that she'd let him know too plainly how important he was to her and doubting that he'd been deceived by that proud declaration of love for Jeremy!

'Oh, by the way, Number Two theatre has been closed for the time being,' Angie remembered to mention.

'There's a fault in the electrical system and it seems we shall have to manage without it for a few days. You can make yourself useful in Recovery, Nurse Lorimer.'

'Yes, Sister. Thank you, Sister.' It was demure, dutiful, but Kelly didn't care for the idea of being banished to the recovery unit when her training and experience could be more usefully employed in any one of the three remaining theatres. But there wasn't anything she could do about it.

As Theatre Sister, Angie had full authority for who did what in her department. Kelly wondered if she was trying to ensure that a nurse she regarded as a rival saw little of any of the surgeons. Including Griff and Jeremy. Didn't she know that Jeremy was away until Tuesday? Or that she had absolutely nothing to fear from any encounter between Griff and a theatre nurse who meant nothing at all to him?

Emerging from the changing-room some ten minutes later, tucking stray strands of soft pale hair into her theatre cap, Kelly saw Griff in the corridor. He was so tall and lean and darkly handsome in the surgical trousers and tunic and so dear that her heart turned over in her breast . . . the foolish heart that must learn to stop loving him and concentrate on caring for the man she was soon to marry, she told herself sternly.

He seemed to be waiting for someone. Maybe herself, she thought with a little leap of optimism. Kelly didn't know whether she should stop and speak or walk past in apparent indifference to punish him for the way he'd virtually ignored her in the office. She was hurt and angry and confused and she decided to pass him without granting him even a smile.

She approached him with a slightly militant sparkle in her hazel eyes. Griff spoke as she drew level.

'Just a minute, Kelly!' It was autocratic, slightly impatient, as he realised that she was about to pass him without a word.

Her chin shot up at the peremptory tone. She loved him but she didn't have to like his arrogance, she thought proudly, briefly forgetting that it was out-weighed by so many things that she did like and admire in the clever and caring and dedicated surgeon.

'A minute is all I can give you,' she said briskly, tone and manner rebuking him for the hurtful attitude that had surely delighted the jealous theatre sister.

Amusement flickered in the grey eyes. 'It's all I need,' he drawled. 'For the moment, anyway. How are you?'

The beginning of a blush dawned in her pretty face, for his voice softened and became intimate and almost caressing on the enquiry. He sounded like a lover, caring and concerned. Kelly didn't want to be reminded by the way he looked and spoke of something that should never have happened. But her heart and body quickened in that most clinical of surroundings.

'I'm fine, thanks. Why shouldn't I be?' she returned, slightly defensive, afraid of betraying relief and delight that he wasn't so indifferent, after all.

'It was a foul night. There's a lot of damage along the coast, apparently. I was anxious about you,' he told her frankly. 'I almost came to rescue you and insist that you spend the night within four strong walls. I had visions of that flimsy van being smashed to smithereens with you inside it. But perhaps you *weren't* inside it? Maybe you spent the night with Hunt?' It was light but probing.

'I didn't.' The blush deepened.

'I'm glad.' He smiled down at her suddenly, a glow in the grey eyes that warmed her heart. 'I think I'd have torn him limb from limb if you'd gone straight to his arms from mine, Kelly.' It was very light but there was something in his tone that told her that he was very much in earnest in his dislike of the thought of her in another man's embrace.

'You forget that I'm engaged to him,' she said, a trifle unsteadily.

'*You* may have forgotten it for a short time,' he said bluntly. 'I never did. It's very much on my mind at this moment. You and I have to talk, Kelly. Oh, not here! This place is much too public. When can I see you? As I expect you heard, I've an appointment this evening . . .'

'With Angie,' she agreed dryly, interrupting him impulsively. 'She should make up her mind which of you she wants. You or Jeremy!'

Observing the slight flush of anger in her face, Griff decided not to explain that he would be spending the evening with Angie and a few hundred other people at the Porthbryn Town Hall, attending a protest meeting about a chemical works, with all its attendant dangers and discharge of effluent into the sea, that was proposed for a site just along the coast and too near the town. He felt that a little jealousy might overcome some of the pride that was threatening to spoil what they had going for each other.

'Well, if you won't let her have Jeremy she might decide to settle for me,' he drawled. 'And I might settle for Angie. Is that what you want?'

Kelly managed a shrug, disconcerted by the gleam of sardonic amusement in his smiling eyes. 'It doesn't really matter to me,' she lied. 'And I really haven't the time to discuss it . . .'

Strong fingers clamped over her slender wrist as she began to turn away. Ignoring the interested gaze of a nurse who came out into the corridor from one of the ante-rooms, he said, low but firmly, 'Then we'll discuss it tomorrow. At length. I gather that Hunt has gone off for a few days. Taken to the hills at the threat of your imminent arrival on his doorstep, no doubt. I assume that you won't be moving, bag and baggage, this weekend? So I'll know where to find you.'

'Don't come looking, Griff,' she said, low and determined, remembering the still-throbbing wound of that murmur of love for Kate and telling herself firmly not to take him seriously. She just couldn't trust him not to hurt her again and again. 'I told you the other day that Hartlake nurses don't make mistakes. That wasn't quite right. I should have said that they don't make the same mistake twice!'

His eyes narrowed. 'Meaning that yesterday was a mistake, Kelly?'

She forced herself to nod. 'Yes . . .'

Griff frowned, unconvinced. 'The only mistake was mine in supposing that you meant what you said and letting you send me away,' he told her forcefully. 'I should have known better. You're proud and stubborn and you have a strong sense of misguided loyalty that will ruin four lives if you aren't very careful. You look as if you haven't slept for thinking about me and I certainly haven't slept for thinking about you. I'm not sure where we go from here, Kelly. But it isn't separate ways, I promise you!'

Her heart shook, stumbled, filled with new hope and new dreams at the look in his eyes and the warmth of the quiet and resolute words. But she still hesitated to believe that he could mean all that he said, all that he implied.

'I don't think I want to go anywhere with you, Griff,' she said proudly. 'I'm not prepared to be second best in any man's life and I know I could never mean half as much as Kate still does.'

'Are you still thrusting Kate down my throat?' He sighed. 'Do I have to live with your cousin for the rest of my life? How do I convince someone as stubborn as you that I really want you . . . with all my heart?'

'You could try not calling me *Katy* when I'm lying in your arms,' she said with sudden bitterness, whisking her wrist from his loosened hold as the approach of a trolley with recumbent patient and attendant porter and ward nurse provided her with an opportunity to escape.

Nurses never ran except in an emergency, but she walked very quickly towards the sanctuary of the recovery unit, furious with the impulsive tongue that had uttered words that had been searing her heart and burning in her brain all night.

But why shouldn't he know how much he'd hurt her? And what was the point of pretending that she didn't love him when he seemed to know it only too well . . .

Kelly was thankful that their paths didn't cross for the rest of the day. He was operating on his scheduled list and she was fully occupied with the patients who came from surgery into recovery for special observation until they were returned to the ward or, in some cases, transferred to the intensive care unit.

She was very busy but she still had time to think about that encounter with Griff and to ponder over his astonishing words. It hurt that he still spoke of 'wanting' when she ached so desperately to have him mention 'loving' and 'needing' and 'staying together'. *With all my heart*, he'd said. But if that heart still belonged to Kate then what happiness was there for any other woman who loved him? Particularly for Kelly, who was a constant reminder of the past with her distinctive likeness to the girl he'd nearly married?

She wished she could trust him not to hurt and disappoint her. But she didn't feel that loving as she now knew it played any part in Griff's life these days, and without that kind of love and a real promise for the

SIGH FOR A SURGEON

future, she couldn't take chances with her happiness.

At the same time, what happiness was there for her if she married a man she didn't love?

As if to atone for the wind and rain and chill of the past week, Saturday dawned bright and fair with the promise of a warm and sunny day.

Kelly pottered about the caravan, doing a few chores, having no plans for the weekend but not wanting to go far in case Griff did turn up as he'd threatened. She was torn between the longing to see him and the determination to send him away if he came.

The Mini was still out of action. She telephoned the garage from the nearby call box and Len Williams agreed to send one of his lads along that afternoon to have a look at it.

Needing a few items from the shop, Kelly took her purse and strolled the hundred yards or so to make her purchases, her long hair lifting in the slight, balmy breeze and the sun warm on bare arms and legs. If Griff or Len's lad should arrive in her absence, it would be obvious that she intended to be away from the caravan for only a few minutes, she decided.

The little shop was busy, for it was run by a talkative spinster who enjoyed a gossip with her customers.

Kelly had no objection to waiting. Amused by the flow of exchanged information that she listened to with half an ear, she stood by a revolving book-stand and browsed through the paperbacks and eventually chose a couple of her favourite authors, slipping the books into the metal shopping basket that hung from her arm.

She was keeping an eye on the traffic that came from the direction of Penbryn, hoping to see a distinctive dark blue car driven by a distinctive dark-haired surgeon. So she saw the huge articulated lorry in the distance long before it rumbled noisily past the shop at speed. She was on her way to the counter with her basket of purchases when she heard the unmistakable sound of air brakes hastily applied and then the loud squeal of tyres and a resounding crash.

With her heart in her mouth, Kelly rushed for the door, followed more slowly and rather doubtfully by the shopkeeper and one or two of her customers. An accident would need the services of a skilled nurse and she was ready to do what she could, although she dreaded the sight that might meet her startled gaze.

She stared in blank dismay at the lorry and her crumpled Mini and the remains of the shattered caravan. It took only seconds to realise that the lorry had left the road and careered through the hedge and into the field, catching the side of the Mini *en route* and spinning it into the road in the path of oncoming traffic. It was in a sorry state, with its shattered windscreen and crumpled wing and caved-in door. But it was nothing compared to the flimsy firewood that was virtually all that was left of the caravan after the collision with the lorry.

A dark blue car was already braking to a fierce halt and a tall figure was abruptly ejected from the driving seat by sheer force of dread. He headed for the remains of the caravan as fast as his lameness would allow. Instantly, Kelly began to run with the metal basket still dangling from her arm.

He was tearing at the debris with bare hands, grim-faced, when she got to him. The lorry driver was just scrambling out of the cab, blood streaming from a cut on his head, dazed and shaken.

'Griff . . . !' Kelly was breathless from her sprint and desperate to reassure him and his name came out as a gasp.

He spun and she knew she would never forget the look in his eyes as he realised that she was not only alive but unharmed. She dropped the basket, its contents spilling, as he swept her into his arms and buried his face in her flyaway hair.

'Oh, my God, thank God!' he said numbly. 'I thought you were in that lot . . . Kelly, oh, Kelly! My love!'

His arms held her so thankfully, she felt the race of his heart and the tension of that terrible anxiety and the flood of relief that made him almost incoherent. 'I'm all right,' she soothed, stroking the crisp black curls. 'Griff, I'm all right . . . I wasn't even here.'

He lifted his head. 'No—where the hell were you?' It was an almost angry, natural reaction.

'In the shop . . . shopping. I'd just gone across the road . . .' Kelly was reacting, too, beginning to shake and feel sick as she realised how lucky an escape she'd had—just because she'd chosen that particular moment to walk down the road for bread and sugar and cheese. If she'd been in or around the van, she couldn't have stood a chance of escaping death or serious injury.

Others had reached the scene. The farmer and his wife. People who'd been in the shop. Passing motorists who'd stopped to offer assistance. Recovering from the first shock, the lorry-driver was voluble, more bitter than hurt, and ready to blame the haulage company who employed him for a steering fault in the lorry rather than himself for not realising it sooner and keeping his speed within the legal limit.

Griff held Kelly very close, very tight. 'If I'd lost you . . . God, it doesn't bear thinking about,' he said roughly. He pressed his lean, scarred cheek against the pale wing of her hair and his tall body trembled with the force of his shaken emotions. 'I knew I loved you but I didn't realise how much . . .' He added on a surge of sudden fury, 'I've never liked this for you, never!'

The sweep of his hand took in the caravan, the coast

road with its constant stream of traffic, the lumbering cows at the far end of the field, Kelly's youth and prettiness and vulnerability. But no one could have foreseen the accident, although his words of only yesterday when he'd spoken of having a vision of the van smashed to smithereens seemed strangely prophetic.

Mrs Evans touched Kelly on the arm, anxious. 'Are you all right? Not hurt, is it? Such a fright we had, seeing that old lorry hurtling through the hedge! There's shocking what can happen when you least expect it, isn't it!'

Kelly drew herself from Griff's tenderly protective arms. 'I'm fine, really,' she assured the kindly and concerned Welshwoman. 'I wasn't in the van. I was over the road. In the shop. I'm all right, Mrs Evans.'

'I'll take care of Miss Lorimer,' Griff said firmly. 'I'm a doctor. She's just shocked.'

Kelly smiled at him, heart in her eyes. 'I think one of us should have a look at that man's head. He's bleeding quite badly, Griff. You can take care of me later.'

'I mean to be doing it for the rest of my life,' he told her in his direct fashion.

Kelly's heart filled with pure happiness. She knew he would never say what he didn't mean. To be able to look forward to a future with a man like Griff, knowing herself loved and needed, surrounded by his true and tender concern and affection and strength for the rest of her life was almost more happiness than any woman had the right to know, she felt.

Mrs Evans beamed on the couple as they moved towards her husband and the lorry-driver who was staunching his cut head with a towel that had been whipped from Kelly's makeshift washing line by the lorry's advance towards the caravan. 'There's romantic,' she murmured warmly.

The police arrived while Griff was administering to

the lorry-driver's head, summoned by the elderly woman who ran the shop. Kelly was thankful that Griff was there to help her deal with the numerous questions, the problem of the battered Mini and the business of rescuing what could be salvaged from the debris of the caravan . . . some of her clothes, a few personal possessions, the framed photograph of Jeremy with its glass incredibly intact.

She'd almost forgotten Jeremy . . .

CHAPTER FOURTEEN

CURLED UP on the sofa in his dressing-gown, hair falling softly about the face that was slightly flushed from the bath he'd insisted on running for her when they finally reached the cottage, Kelly cradled a mug of fragrant coffee and smiled at the surgeon who'd taken such tender loving care of her in the last few hours. It all seemed like a dream, she thought happily. Something like the dream she'd cherished for so many years about a man who she hadn't really expected ever to see again but would recognise as her destiny if he came back into her life.

Griff put out a hand to cradle her small head in a brief, loving gesture. He stroked the long, pale fall of her hair. 'I love you,' he said softly.

Kelly's heart moved in her breast. She turned her head to kiss the strong, clever fingers as they rested against her cheek. She sighed. 'I love you. But you knew that days ago . . .'

He shook his dark head. 'I may have seemed that confident but I wasn't, Kelly. I hoped but I didn't know. And I was scared to death that you'd marry Hunt despite anything I could say or do. I knew I didn't want that to happen. I knew I needed you. Now I know that I wouldn't care about anything if I lost you . . .' He broke off on a sudden surge of emotion that threatened to unman him, a weakness of loving that only made him more of a man in her eyes.

Kelly leaned to kiss the sensual mouth, to murmur once more, 'I love you . . .'

'Then let's not have any more nonsense about marrying Jeremy,' he said sternly. 'You're going to marry me.' His tone brooked no argument in the matter.

'Yes,' she said, meek before that masterful note in his deep, dear voice. There was no hesitation and no apprehension in this man's clear-cut decision for the future, she realised. Not like Jeremy, who'd never wanted to marry her and had been coerced into an engagement and talk of wedding plans. That wasn't loving. Loving was this man's need to have her by his side until the end of time. Loving was this man's longing to surround her with his love and tender concern and protective strength for as long as they both should live. Loving was the mutual certainty that only marriage with its special bonding and welcomed ties and responsibilities could crown their happiness in each other. 'Oh, yes,' she said again, happily.

Griff took the mug from her unresisting fingers and set it down on the low table. He smiled into the hazel eyes with their endearing honesty and drew her into his arms, cradling her tenderly. His lips trailed a route via soft hair and smooth brow and curved eyelids and shapely nose and delicately flushed cheek to the sweet and tremulous and warmly responsive mouth.

Kelly's arms tightened convulsively about him as their lips finally met and clung. Her heart raced and senses swirled and her whole being was filled with a wonderful, glowing faith in a future they were destined to share.

She drew his hand to her breast and held it there in shy but eager invitation and she caught her breath on a swift, sharp ache of longing as he began to caress her, quickening with a desire that leaped to match the sudden flame in him.

Griff made slow, sensuous and very tender love to her and his lovemaking held all the magic and all the enchantment of a previous occasion—but now there was much deeper meaning for them both in the delight they brought to each other. For the knowledge and the frank confession of mutual love enriched every kiss, every touch, every moment of intimate and ecstatic embrace.

Afterwards they talked, making plans, dreaming dreams, and the conversation was interspersed with the little kisses and smiles and tender words of lovers since time began.

The idyll was interrupted by the persistent shrill of the telephone. Griff reluctantly reached to lift the receiver from its cradle, hoping it wasn't an urgent call from the hospital. He wasn't duty surgeon but sometimes his special skills and experience were needed to deal with an emergency.

He sat up suddenly, tensing. 'Has he, by God! Is it bad? How bad? All right, Angie, I'll be there right away. Yes . . . yes, I'll tell her. Yes, she's here with me. Oh, you heard about that? She's all right, yes, fine. Okay, Angie . . . I'm on my way!' He hung up, turned to Kelly.

She closed her eyes briefly against all that she thought she saw in his handsome, concerned face. 'It's Jeremy, isn't it?' she said, stricken. 'Something's happened to him . . .'

'He's alive,' Griff said quickly, answering the unspoken dread in the way she looked and spoke. 'He's had a fall. No great distance but he landed badly, apparently. On some rocks. The emergency services rushed him to the Porthbryn General as the nearest A and E hospital and someone rang Angie. She's there now.'

'How bad is he? Does she say he'll do?' The traditional term for patients expected to make a full recovery from illness or surgery leaped automatically to her lips as she hastily left the rumpled bed and began to hunt for the clothes she'd left in the bedroom prior to her bath. 'Angie sounded dreadful . . .' The shrill, desperate tones had carried distinctly over the wire, although she hadn't been able to make any sense of the incoherent words. Somehow, she hadn't needed to hear them to know what Angie was saying.

'She's very shocked. She's very much in love with him, Kelly.' He was already dressing, thrusting long legs into slacks, pulling a sweater over rumpled black curls with the practised speed of a man who'd spent years of his life answering emergency calls at all hours of the day and night.

Kelly nodded. 'I think I knew that.' She reached for the thin blue frock that had seemed so suitable for a warm day and scrambled into it, fastening buttons with unsteady fingers. 'How bad is he?' she asked again.

He didn't attempt to hide anything from her. 'Fractured spine and pelvis. Both legs broken. He's in the theatre right now. Fleming is duty surgeon. We both know he likes to take his time but he's thorough, Kelly. He'll do a good job.' It was reassuring.

'Yes, of course. That doesn't sound too bad,' she said bravely, knowing as he did that it might be very, very bad. There was never any telling with spinal damage and so much depended on which of the vertebrae had suffered in the fall. She closed her mind to the thought of all the complications and problems that might arise from a back injury.

Jeremy was an experienced climber. How had he come to fall any distance—and hadn't he been wearing a safety-harness? How long had it taken the emergency services to reach him? Had anything been done in the meantime? Had his friends attempted to move him and caused more damage? Would Henry Fleming do a good job? How long would it be before he was well again? So many questions sped through Kelly's mind as she hurried out of the house in Griff's wake.

In the car she was silent, hands gripped tensely in her lap as he drove towards Porthbryn and the hospital. They passed Caradoc Farm and the lingering evidence of that earlier accident in which, fortunately, no one had been badly hurt. Her Mini had been towed away to the garage in Penbryn. The police had organised the removal of the lorry. Pieces of broken glass and hardboard littered the field in silent memorial to the caravan that she'd called home for a few weeks. The cows had at last been moved from the field with its broken-down hedge.

Kelly gave it all the merest of indifferent glances in passing. All her thoughts, all her concern, were for Jeremy.

Griff turned his dark head to look at the small, set face of the girl he loved so dearly and then he reached to cover the tightly clasped hands with one of his own. 'Darling, don't get swept away by emotion, will you?' he said quietly, anxious to protect his newfound happiness and convinced that her happiness lay with him. But he knew her warm impulsiveness, her obstinacy, her strangely misguided sense of loyalty and dreaded where they all might lead her. 'No matter what, we belong together. I love you and I need you, Kelly.'

She stiffened at his touch, at the meaningful words. 'Griff, please! I can't even think about us at the moment,' she said, almost desperately.

She couldn't bear to face the thought that she might have to do something that would hurt them both. Something unavoidable. Something that strangely seemed to have been inevitable since she first came to Porthbryn. Jeremy was badly hurt. Jeremy's back was broken. Jeremy might never walk again. Despite all that had

happened between herself and Griff, she was still engaged to Jeremy, she thought bleakly. How could she do
to him what Kate had once done to Griff in strikingly
similar circumstances?

It was unthinkable for someone like herself . . .

Angie seemed calmer by the time they reached the
hospital and Theatres. But there was a terrible bleakness
in the dark eyes as she moved towards Griff and into his
outstretched arms. He held her close, comforting and
reassuring. Knowing that it held nothing more than the
affection of long and warm association, Kelly still didn't
look on that embrace with any liking. Yet she was sorry
for Angie, who seemed to love Jeremy as she never had.
He was her very dear friend. He was Angie's reason for
living.

Jeremy was still in the operating theatre, undergoing
surgery to place his fractured spine in traction and to set
his broken pelvis and legs and put them into extensive
plaster. After a brief exchange with Angie, Griff went
away to don green trousers and tunic and gown and
mask. He wouldn't be needed to assist his colleague, but
he was anxious to find out the extent of injury and the
probable prognosis and report back to the waiting
women.

Angie didn't speak to Kelly. She seemed to be dis-
orientated, wandering about the small sitting-room,
picking up things and putting them down without
apparently knowing what her hands were doing. It was
surprising for such a cool and capable theatre sister to go
to pieces so completely. But Kelly felt that Angie could
have handled the situation so much better if she'd been
on duty and kept busy with the running of Theatres. As it
was, she had nothing to do but wait and worry and
expect the worst. Like herself.

Theatre staff drifted in and out of the room at intervals

with reassuring remarks. A nurse brought them both some tea and biscuits. There seemed to be a great deal of sympathy for Angie and none at all for her, Kelly thought wryly. Yet everyone knew that she was supposed to be marrying Jeremy very soon. Had it always been so apparent that she didn't really love him? And had she been suspected of taking him away from Angie out of spite? Or was it only that Angie was so much better known and better liked than a newcomer who was still something of an unknown quantity to the staff of the Porthbryn General?

'Shall I pour tea for you, Angie?' Kelly tried to bring some normality to the situation with the quiet words. It was absurd that Angie should be so stricken and wringing her hands for *her* fiancé while Kelly sat quietly pouring tea as though she didn't care. She *did* care. She was desperately anxious for Jeremy and his future . . . a future that might be irrevocably linked with her own. For if the loving was all on Angie's side and Jeremy had been perfectly happy with their engagement and marriage plans and loved her still, then he would need her more than ever in the months to come. Particularly if he learned that he would never walk again . . .

Angie looked at her blankly for a moment. Then she said, 'I thought Griff would know where you were.' It was said too dully to be malicious.

A little colour crept into Kelly's face. 'I've known him a very long time,' she said defensively.

'He told me.' It was colourless. 'You were going to marry him, weren't you? Years ago.'

'No. That was my cousin.'

'Oh, yes. Kate. He talks about her in his sleep sometimes. I expect you know.'

Kelly's hands clenched convulsively at the casually dropped information that Angie had shared some nights with the surgeon and at the implication that she was assumed to have done the same since her arrival in Porthbryn. She thought wryly that no one would believe that she'd been a virgin before she'd succumbed to the magic and the ecstasy of Griff's embrace.

'No,' she said stiffly. 'I didn't know.'

'Well, he does.'

'Kate hurt him rather badly.'

'Now you want to do the same.' Angie sat down suddenly just as if her legs had refused to support her any longer.

There wasn't a scrap of real interest in her tone, Kelly realised. The theatre sister was merely making conversation to pass the desolate minutes until there was news of Jeremy's condition. But it seemed that the usually reserved Griff had confided in Angie to some extent.

'I don't want to hurt anyone,' she said carefully, meaning it. 'Not Griff. Not you. Least of all Jeremy. I'm very fond of Jeremy.'

'Fond?' Angie's lip curled slightly. For the first time, there was a hint of animation in the pale face. 'And you think that's good enough reason for taking him from me? I love him!'

Kelly looked at her levelly. 'I didn't take him from you, Angie. He loved me long before he even met you,' she said, making it as gentle as she could.

'Did you sleep with him? He would never say.' She gestured almost helplessly as Kelly stiffened. 'Oh, don't bother to answer. It doesn't matter now, anyway. Nothing matters as long as . . . as he's all right.' Her voice broke on the words.

Kelly saw the tears start and stream unchecked down the girl's face and her heart contracted with an impulsive compassion. 'He will be,' she said firmly, with a confi-

dence she didn't really feel. 'Jeremy is very resilient.
He's the type who bounces back no matter how hard life
slaps him down.'

The words were well-meaning but they created an
unfortunate visual image. Angie began to laugh in the
midst of tears, close to hysteria. 'He should have
bounced off those bloody rocks!'

Kelly cursed her clumsiness. Hastily, she got to her
feet and took Angie by the shoulders and shook her
sternly. 'Now that's enough!' she declared, almost
angry. 'Pull yourself together! If Jeremy could see and
hear you now he'd think himself at death's door! And he
isn't! Nowhere near it!'

It was effective. Angie gasped and stopped crying,
controlled the gusting and humourless laughter. 'Oh,'
she said weakly, breathlessly, feeling foolish, 'I'm sorry.
I didn't mean to thrust that on you!'

'Never mind.' Kelly resumed her seat and picked up
the teapot and poured tea for herself and the theatre
sister. 'I do know how you feel,' she said quietly. 'I love
him too, you know.' Not as Angie loved him, perhaps.
Not as she loved Griff. But surely enough to give up a
dream for the reality that might be Jeremy's love and
Jeremy's need, she told herself firmly.

Griff came abruptly into the room, pulling off the
theatre cap, mask dangling by its green tapes about his
neck. Both girls turned to him, eager but apprehensive.
'He's out of surgery and he's come round sufficiently to
confirm that there's no brain damage. They've taken
him along to ICU. He'll do.'

It was Angie he addressed. It was Kelly who leaped to
her feet and headed for the door. 'They'll let me see him,
won't they?'

'Darling, he won't be conscious,' he said gently.

'I know that!'

'He isn't a pretty sight, Kelly. He broke his nose and gashed his face badly in the fall and he's a mass of bruises.'

'As if that matters,' she said impatiently and hurried from the room.

Angie looked at Griff. 'I don't have any rights, do I?' she said heavily. '*I'm* not engaged to him.'

He put an arm about her slim shoulders, hugged her. 'Nor will Kelly be for much longer if I have any say in the matter,' he said firmly. 'I won't let her marry Jeremy. That's a promise.' He made the promise as much to himself as to Angie. For Kelly was far too important to him to allow her to make a noble and totally unnecessary sacrifice of the happiness of four people . . .

Kelly looked down at Jeremy, heart wrenching. He was suspended in traction and encased in plaster, almost unrecognisable but for the auburn hair that had been shaved away in places for the traction bolts to be inserted into his skull. She bent to touch her lips to the bruised face and then stepped back and out of the way as a nurse came to the bedside to make the half-hourly observations.

She sent up a silent prayer for him and turned to leave, knowing there was nothing she could do for him. Dear Jeremy, with his warmth and sweetness and good-natured desire to please everyone and hurt no one, she thought wryly. If only she loved him just a little more and Griff a whole lot less . . .

Griff was waiting for her, tall and darkly handsome and very dear. He held out his hand to her, a special smile that held a plea as much as love in the deep-set eyes. 'Come on, darling. I'll take you home.'

Kelly shook her head. 'I'm not coming back with you, Griff,' she said with a resolution that overcame the appeal of the quiet words.

His eyes narrowed. 'There's nothing you can do here, Kelly. He won't even know that you're around . . .'

'I'm going to the flat. Jeremy's flat. I'll stay there for a few days. It's what I planned to do, you know.'

'What good do you think that will do anyone?' he demanded angrily.

'I don't know. But I can't be with you, not yet. Not until . . .' She broke off, biting her lip.

'Until you've made up your mind whether you love me or Hunt?'

'Don't make it hard for me, Griff.'

'I intend to make it impossible for you,' he told her grimly. 'I know what's in your mind, Kelly. But the circumstances are different, you know. Tell Hunt that you don't want to marry him and you'll be doing both him and Angie a favour!'

Kelly began to walk to the lift, strain showing in her face. 'You don't *know* that, Griff. Nor do I.'

'You're as stubborn as a mule!'

'I have to be sure,' she said mulishly.

In the lift, Griff put his arms about her. 'Don't do this to me, Kelly,' he said, low and urgent. 'We have something special, something rare. Don't throw it away for a man who'll need love, not pity, if he comes out of this in the same shape as I was, six years ago. You've never understood that although it hurt, I didn't want Kate to marry me if she couldn't love me whole or half a man. Try to believe that I *know* what Hunt will want. I've been there, Kelly. I know what I'm talking about.'

She allowed him to hold her, needing the strong arms to keep her from sinking into a sea of despair. 'I have to do what I feel is right.'

He swept the silken mass of hair from her face and cradled her small head with a tender hand. '*This* is right. You and me. Anything else is totally wrong.' He laid his warm lips on the sweet, stubborn mouth and kissed her with a wealth of loving.

She sighed and clung to him briefly before the lift doors opened. He was persuasive and she loved him. But she had to resist the promise of happiness that he offered until she knew how necessary she was to Jeremy's recovery and return to health and mobility. She couldn't play fast and loose with his life and his heart, even if her own had to sigh for a surgeon she loved and could have married, for the rest of her life . . .

For three days she stayed at Jeremy's flat, surrounded by reminders of him, while he lay in traction, heavily sedated to ease the pain that was a good indication that there was little fear of permanent paralysis.

He drifted in and out of consciousness, unaware of his surroundings or the untiring ministrations of the unit nurses or the visits that Kelly and Angie made at different times during those days. Both girls were waiting for some sign of what the future held for them. Anxiety and uncertainty created a kind of bond between a theatre sister and a nurse who could never be friends but had a mutual interest in the fate and the feelings of the young surgeon, and they kept each other informed as to his progress.

It was a busy time in Theatres and they were both glad to have plenty to occupy their minds and hands, even if their hearts couldn't set aside concern for Jeremy. Number Two Theatre was back in use by Wednesday after an extensive check of the electrical circuits and Kelly was getting it ready for a laparotomy, expecting Griff and steeling herself to work with him in such close contact, when Angie came unexpectedly into the ante-room.

'I've just had a call from ICU,' she said, a hint of triumph as well as challenge in the way she looked and spoke. 'Jeremy's asking for me . . .'

Kelly felt as though an enormous burden had rolled away from her heart. 'I'm glad,' she said simply.

Angie nodded. 'I believe you are,' she said. 'And I meant to fight you tooth and nail for him, Kelly!'

It was the first time that the theatre sister had used her first name. Kelly smiled at her warmly. 'There isn't any need, is there? Now we both know what Jeremy wants. Give him my love and tell him that I'm going to marry Griff. He'll be happy for me.'

When Griff arrived some minutes later, she went to meet him, love leaping in her heart for the surgeon who'd almost suffered a second time through loving a Lorimer. She felt that he'd proved in the last few days how much he loved her and she meant to spend the rest of her life showing how much she loved and needed him.

'So you're my scrub nurse this morning. Good!' he greeted her, smiling.

'We make a good team,' she reminded him lightly.

He nodded. 'I'm still hoping to keep it that way.' He touched her soft cheek in a brief, tender caress that spoke of love and need. His touch, his tone and the aching anxiety in his grey eyes told Kelly that he hadn't yet heard that Jeremy had roused and reached out for the woman he really wanted.

'So am I. But I'm not sure if you want your wife to carry on working,' she said with deceptive demureness.

She heard the little catch of his breath as the words and their meaning registered. Then he took her into his arms and kissed her, disregarding all the rules that insisted a surgeon shouldn't kiss a scrub nurse in a sterile theatre. Even if they did belong together for ever and always . . .

Doctor Nurse Romances

Amongst the intense emotional pressures of modern medical life, doctors and nurses often find romance. Read about their lives and loves in the other three Doctor Nurse titles available this month.

SISTER IN A SARONG
by Jenny Ashe
The Garden of Eden — that's Sister Eve Carrol's first impression of the plantation hospital in Malaysia. But she soon uncovers problems in paradise when she incurs the displeasure of her handsome boss, Dr Andrew Craig...

A TIME TO HEAL
by Sarah Franklin
Impervious to feminine charms — that's the rumour about surgeon Stuart Lyndon. Which is fine by Lisa Dawson, his quiet and reserved scrub nurse, who steers well clear of personal relationships. So why is it that of all the willing nurses at St Jude's it's *she* who catches Mr Lyndon's eye?

NURSE IN WAITING
by Janet Ferguson
Forced by injury to take a break from nursing, Thea Westering counts herself lucky to land a secretarial job on St Stephen's orthopaedic ward. And even luckier to work with attractive registrar James Mayling...

Mills & Boon
the rose of romance

Mills & Boon

4 Doctor Nurse Romances
FREE

Coping with the daily tragedies and ordeals of a busy hospital, and sharing the satisfaction of a difficult job well done, people find themselves unexpectedly drawn together. Mills & Boon Doctor Nurse Romances capture perfectly the excitement, the intrigue and the emotions of modern medicine, that so often lead to overwhelming and blissful love. By becoming a regular reader of Mills & Boon Doctor Nurse Romances you can enjoy EIGHT superb new titles every two months plus a whole range of special benefits: your very own personal membership card, a free newsletter packed with recipes, competitions, bargain book offers, plus big cash savings.

AND an Introductory FREE GIFT for YOU.
Turn over the page for details.

**Fill in and send this coupon back today
and we'll send you**

4 Introductory
Doctor Nurse Romances yours to keep
FREE

At the same time we will reserve a
subscription to Mills & Boon
Doctor Nurse Romances for you. Every
two months you will receive the latest
8 new titles, delivered direct to your door.
You don't pay extra for delivery. Postage and
packing is always completely Free.
There is no obligation or commitment –
you receive books only for
as long as you want to.

**It's easy! Fill in the coupon below and return it to
MILLS & BOON READER SERVICE, FREEPOST, P.O. BOX 236,
CROYDON, SURREY CR9 9EL.**

**Please note: READERS IN SOUTH AFRICA write to
Mills & Boon Ltd., Postbag X3010,
Randburg 2125, S. Africa.**

- -

FREE BOOKS CERTIFICATE

**To: Mills & Boon Reader Service, FREEPOST, P.O. Box 236,
Croydon, Surrey CR9 9EL.**

Please send me, free and without obligation, four Dr. Nurse Romances, and reserve a
Reader Service Subscription for me. If I decide to subscribe I shall receive, following my free
parcel of books, eight new Dr. Nurse Romances every two months for £8.00, post and
packing free. If I decide not to subscribe, I shall write to you within 10 days. The free books
are mine to keep in any case. I understand that I may cancel my subscription at any time
simply by writing to you. I am over 18 years of age.
Please write in BLOCK CAPITALS.

Name _____

Address _____

_____

_____ Postcode _____

SEND NO MONEY — TAKE NO RISKS

*Remember, postcodes speed delivery. Offer applies in UK only and is not valid to
present subscribers. Mills & Boon reserve the right to exercise discretion
in granting membership. If price changes are necessary you will be noti-
fied. Offer expires 30th June 1985.*

8DN

EP11